The Mice of the Round Table

A Tail of Camelot

Julie Leung

Piccadilly
PRESS

First published in Great Britain in 2016 by
PICCADILLY PRESS
80–81 Wimpole St, London W1G 9RE
www.piccadillypress.co.uk

A CIP catalogue record for this book
is available from the British Library.

ISBN: 978-1-84812-513-1
also available as an ebook

1

Typeset by Palimpsest Book Production Limited,
Falkirk, Stirlingshire

Printed and bound by Clays Ltd, St Ives Plc

Piccadilly Press is an imprint of Bonnier Zaffre Ltd,
a Bonnier Publishing company
www.bonnierpublishing.co.uk

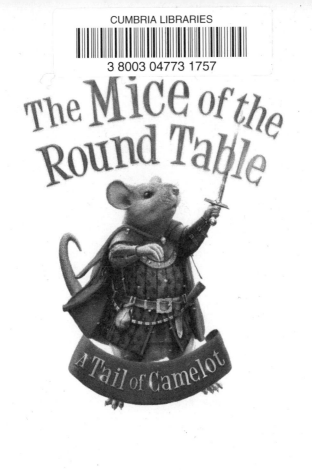

The Mice of the Round Table

Round Table

A Tail of Camelot

For Kyle:
I'll have you, Longshanks.

'We lived in a land destined to become myth. Powers walked the realm in those days, forces which are now gone from the earth. How or why, I cannot say. But you know that it is true.'

– Roger Zelazny,
The Last Defender of Camelot

Prologue

Macie Cornwall leaped from one tree branch to the next, keeping a wary eye on the winged shadow as it moved closer to the open fields that marked Camelot's borders. The owl's wingspan nearly blotted out the sun as the bird passed overhead. The young squirrel narrowed her eyes.

The Darkling Woods possessed secret ways of warning. To those who knew how to listen, they had many important things to tell. Macie knew this better than most. For as long as she had patrolled the forest, she had been able to decipher its language. Her da, who patrolled as head scout before her, had taught her well.

The low chirping from the crickets meant a long, frigid winter ahead. The thickness of moss on the rowan trees predicted the inches of the first snowfall. Too many speckled moths meant a slim harvest. The creatures that called these green wilds home existed in a delicate balance. If something disturbed the order, there were signs all around.

When she reached the highest bough on a giant elm, Macie found the vantage point she needed. Her ear tufts twitched as she gauged the wind's direction. She retrieved an arrow from her quiver and notched it into her reed bow. Setting the bow against her arm bracer and pulling the string taut, Macie lined up a warning shot to whizz past the horned owl's left ear.

'Too close to home, birdbrain,' she whispered.

Before she could release the arrow, the owl was joined in the air by a fledgling brood. There were three in all; the owlets were just shedding the fluff of their nest days. Flying shakily, they followed their mother as she banked to the south, away from Camelot and towards the ruins of St Gertrude. The top of the church's blackened steeple peeked above the trees.

Macie exhaled and lowered her bow, wiping the sweat from her paws. She was relieved to have avoided a confrontation. But a larger worry had wormed into her heart.

This was the third owl flock she had seen take flight at midday in the past month. And the Owls of Fellwater Swamps did not venture outside their territory without good reason, especially not during the day.

It was an omen of great change. Macie did not know what exactly it foretold; she only knew that she did not like it.

Chapter One

The red hawthorn berry flew at Calib Christopher faster than he could dodge it. Swallowing back a squeak, the mouse gripped the wooden toothpick tighter in his paws and swung down as hard as he could.

Thwack!

Calib struck the berry mere inches away from his snout. It broke in half, splattering his face with sticky pulp. Breathing heavily, Calib wiped the gunk off his whiskers. He scowled in the direction of the tall brown mouse stationed behind the slingshot.

'Top form, Calib!' Devrin Savortooth cheered.

She picked up another berry and readied it in the sling. 'Now, try leaning sideways from your strike so you don't get sprayed! Remember: don't over-think it!'

Calib shook his head. Five heart-pummelling rounds against the Hurler were more than enough for one morning, and Devrin was launching the targets faster than usual.

'Hold your whiskers!' he yelled back. He dropped his practice sword and raised his paws. 'I need to wash off!'

He walked to the edge of the training ground, which was nestled in a weedy corner of the castle garden. Wetting his paws with dewdrops that had collected on a turnip leaf, he did his best to clean the sticky juice from his fur.

Calib breathed in the late autumn smells of crisp leaves and woodsmoke. The air hummed with excite-ment as the mice of Camelot made their final preparations for the Harvest Tournament. The bustling was a welcome break from a sombre harvest season, full of rumours of possible Darkling attacks. But in the end, the wheat and barley had been collected without any trouble. It was time to celebrate.

This year would be Devrin's first time attempting the three Harvest Tournament challenges to prove her bravery, strength, and wisdom. If she passed, she could begin her career as a squire, go on adventures beyond Camelot's borders, and eventually become a knight.

As an adopted daughter of Camelot, Devrin was eager to prove her worth. She was an orphan, having lost her parents when she was only two years old during the Great War between the creatures of the castle and the creatures of the nearby Darkling Woods. Now ending her third year as a page, Devrin was ready to do her part to defend Camelot.

Calib understood. He couldn't imagine anything more glorious than becoming a knight himself and following in his grandfather's and father's pawsteps to protect their home. Though the Great War had ended ten years ago with a peace treaty between Camelot and the Darkling Woods, there was still deep mistrust. Rumours of restless and raiding Darklings grew each year. It was more important than ever to stay vigilant. Even though Calib was only a second-year page, he also wanted to do his part to be prepared.

He just wished Devrin would channel her excitement into someone else's drills.

Calib eyed the other pages going through their morning exercises. To his left, a timid, brown mouse named Barnaby Twill slashed blindly at the air with his wooden sword. Coaching him was a sprightly, tan mouse with white fur trimming her ears and tail. She wore a chain-mail tunic over her smock. Calib felt a tangle of envy and admiration at the sight of Cecily von Mandrake. The best swords-mouse of all the pages, she patiently gave pointers as she sparred with Barnaby.

'Don't close your eyes! You want to see where you're aiming your blocks!'

Glancing away from Barnaby's awkward parries, Cecily noticed Calib watching.

'Morning, Calib!' She smiled and gave a wave across the arena. 'How's the Hurler this morning?'

'Hi, Ceci,' Calib croaked back.

He was debating whether she really wanted to know about the Hurler or whether she was just being polite, when something coiled tightly around his legs. Off balance, Calib toppled onto all fours in the dirt. He looked down and found his footpaws entangled by a bola – a length of rope with a pebble tied to each end. When thrown, it was meant to trip an unsuspecting target from behind. Calib twisted around and saw Warren Clipping sauntering towards him.

'Sorry about that!' Warren said, barely containing

a smug smile. 'You were staring for so long I mistook you for a target dummy.'

The grey-furred menace had always made Calib's life at Camelot extra difficult. Warren had been especially grating since he'd entered himself into the Harvest Tournament. For the past few months, he hadn't let anyone forget it. Today, he was already dressed in his newly stitched tournament robes.

'I wasn't staring,' Calib protested, dusting himself off. He glanced over to make sure Cecily hadn't overheard. Luckily, her attention had turned back to Barnaby. 'I was just taking a break.'

'A break from the *berries*?' Warren scoffed. 'I thought berries were only for first years. I stopped using them a full year ago.'

Calib's face turned hot under his whiskers. Warren's insults always managed to find their targets. Truth was, Calib dreaded the prospect of facing the harder seeds and nuts. Missing them meant being covered in bruises instead of berry juice.

'As a matter of fact, I was just about to move on to the acorns,' Calib said. 'If you'll excuse me.'

He brushed past Warren and marched back to his place before the Hurler. Picking up his wooden sword, Calib gave a few practise swings as a show of confidence.

'Bring on the acorns!' he called to Devrin, hoping he sounded more fearless than he felt.

'Feeling bold, are we?' Devrin said good-naturedly as she grabbed an acorn to set in the Hurler. 'All right, here comes the first one!'

Calib's stomach clenched as she began pulling the acorn tight against the sling, stretching the fabric to its very limits.

'Uh, Devrin, are you sure you need to—'

The acorn shot across the field. For Calib, the world seemed to slow to a crawl. His muscles froze; his mind went blank. As the nut barrelled straight for Calib's head, he had only one thought: *This is going to hurt.*

The next thing Calib saw were white clouds swimming into focus above him. The left side of his snout blossomed with throbbing pain, and his eyes smarted with tears. The acorn had knocked him flat on his back.

'Rat whiskers! Are you all right, Cal?' Devrin yelled.

Calib blinked to stop the sky from spinning and then slowly sat up. Everyone in the training ground had stopped to stare. Cecily had one paw to her mouth. And Warren was nearly doubled over laughing.

Barnaby ran up to Calib's side and offered to help him up.

'Got bonked pretty good there,' he observed.

'I'm fine! I'm fine!' Calib shooed Barnaby's outstretched paw away like a bothersome fly. He stood up on his own. Woozy and disoriented, he touched his jaw tenderly. Luckily, nothing seemed broken.

'At this rate, Barnaby will be made a squire before you, and he can't even parry without closing his eyes!' Warren jeered. Calib's ears boiled with embarrassment.

Before he could respond, a hawthorn berry smashed into Warren's side. It left a smear of pulp along the length of his new clothes.

'Oops!' Devrin called out, smirking. 'My paw must have slipped.'

Warren turned as red as the juice stains. He opened his month to say something when a brusque voice barked out across the arena.

'At attention, pages!'

Sir Owen Onewhisker entered the far side of the grounds, dressed in a hauberk – a shirt of chain mail. The burly black mouse was Camelot's fiercest hand-to-hand swordsmouse. He had lost most of his whiskers in a duel with a ferret, but he kept his single remaining one oiled and groomed.

Calib and the rest of the mice rushed to form a line in front of him, saluting with their tails.

'I take it you all know the importance of tonight,' Sir Owen said in a gruff tone. As the mouse responsible for combat training, he was known to be hard but fair. 'This evening, three of you ratscallions will be given a chance to prove your qualities and become Camelot squires.'

Mice wishing to compete in the Harvest Tournament had signed up months ago by slipping their names into a locked box outside Sir Owen's workroom. But aside from Devrin and Warren, Calib knew of no other mouse who had declared intentions to participate that year.

While anyone – from the field mice to the kitchen mice – could enter the tournament, most who participated were trained for three years as a page first. Devrin and Warren were the only third-year pages that year.

Calib and the others looked around, wondering who the mystery third contestant might be. Was it Cecily? Calib felt a nibble of jealousy at the possibility.

'It is now your turn to protect Camelot for future

generations. There are creatures out there who would like nothing more than to see this castle fall. Remember, the Darklings were merely driven back – not defeated – in the Great War. If they ever attack again, we must be ready.'

Camelot was always at odds with the loose network of woodland tribes – black squirrels, crows, clever hares, and their ilk. Wild in nature, they refused to rely on Two-Leggers for anything. Of course, when food ran scarce in the forest, their attention turned to their better-fed neighbours. Bad blood festered between the Darklings and Camelot for generations, forcing every kind of creature to choose sides. Only the Owls of the Fellwater Swamps remained neutral.

Many years ago, before Calib was born, the Darkling raids were a common menace. Camelot had been forced to retaliate, beginning a long and costly war – the Great War. It was Calib's father, Sir Trenton, who managed to beat the Darklings back in their final siege of the castle. And it was Calib's grandfather Commander Yvers who forced Leftie the lynx to sign a peace treaty. The Darklings were banned from ever crossing Rickonback River. Leftie Wildfang and his allies retreated to his lair east of the forest, in the foothills of the Iron Mountains.

Sir Owen Onewhisker scanned the row of pages with a shrewd eye. 'We live in peace and plenty because of the sacrifices made by mouse-warriors who came before you.'

Calib straightened his shoulders as he thought of his father.

'After your morning chores, each contestant will report to the armoury to have your armour fitted and inspected,' Sir Owen said, unrolling a scroll of parchment. 'And now, for our contestants.

'Warren Clipping!

'Devrin Savortooth!'

Warren and Devrin each stepped forward as Sir Owen called out their names.

'And our final contender this year is . . . Calib Christopher!'

Chapter Two

It was as if the acorn had smacked Calib in the head a second time. His jaw dropped open. Devrin gave his shoulder a friendly punch.

'You little rat. You didn't tell me you were competing!' she laughed.

Calib's throat went dry as bone. *Who slipped my name into the box?* he wondered, frantic. Devrin and Warren had been training for the tournament for *months*.

The challenges were notoriously dangerous. Just two years ago, a page had burned off all his whiskers in the bravery challenge. And the year before that, poor Lars, the stable mouse, had lost his tail entirely. Worst of all, those who failed the Harvest Tournament didn't get another chance to prove themselves as squires. They had to choose a different path – one that led to the kitchen with Madame von Mandrake, the fields with Farmer Chaff, or another trade entirely.

'There must be a mistake,' Calib whispered to Devrin. 'I – I didn't sign up.'

Devrin frowned. 'What do you mean?'

'I mean someone else must have entered my name . . .' His eyes landed on Warren. The grey mouse smiled back at him, a thin leer that lit up his eyes with cruel amusement.

Warren.

As Sir Owen went over the rest of the day's preparations, Calib was consumed with thoughts of revenge. He could cover Warren's shield with kitchen grease so he couldn't pick it up. Or glue his sword into its sheath. Or put spitfire peppers into his helmet.

But none of these ideas could help him withdraw from the tournament without embarrassing the family name.

As a Christopher, Calib had a lot to live up to. His grandfather was the great Commander Yvers

Christopher, leader of all Camelot's mice. Calib's father, Sir Trenton Christopher, had been a war hero.

'Are you paying attention, Calib?' Sir Owen's voice cut through the mouse's thoughts.

Calib opened his mouth. *Just say it*, a tiny voice urged inside his head. *Back out while you still can.* Warren's smirk was so large that the corner of his mouth was halfway up his snout. A hot spark of anger ignited in Calib. He wouldn't let Warren make him look like a fool again!

'Yes, sir,' Calib lied. Warren gaped at him. Clearly, he had expected Calib to back out.

'Good,' Sir Owen said. 'Then you three are released from training early to attend your morning chores. After breakfast, you will show up at your designated times for your armour fittings. Don't be late.'

Calib was too stunned to speak. Before any of the other mice could question him and demand explanations he couldn't provide, he turned and hurried to the tapestry hall, where his chores waited. Calib barely noticed where he was going along the way. He was too preoccupied with thoughts of Warren, the prank and the tournament he would have to face.

Calib followed a gutter path that cut across the castle gate. The secret passageways that ran throughout the castle were well known to him. They formed an intricate labyrinth from the stone foundations to the rafters, an invisible world where Camelot's mice flourished. Just as he was nearly across the gate, he felt a rumble underneath his paws, like faraway thunder. He looked up just in time to see four horses trotting across the open drawbridge, heading straight for him.

With a squeak of alarm, Calib dashed for the nearest cover he could find, climbing into an empty feeding trough. It wasn't a perfect hiding spot, but at least now the horses wouldn't trample him.

Peeking over the lip of the trough, Calib watched the steeds pass, each carrying an armoured Two-Legger on its back. They were warhorses, all muscle and power, draped in red-and-white silks that matched the Two-Leggers' shields: three diagonal red stripes set against a white background.

Calib recognised that crest immediately. It belonged to Sir Lancelot, the bravest and fiercest of King Arthur's knights, whose feats were renowned among every inhabitant of Camelot. Like most of the Two-Legger knights, Sir Lancelot was supposedly far away, seeking adventure. Even King Arthur

18

himself had departed last month on a quest to the Holy Lands. Calib's nose twitched with excitement. Perhaps Arthur and Lancelot were returning.

With so many human knights gone, Camelot's stores were full of uneaten food. While this was certainly not a bad thing, the abundance of crops also made the castle a target for the creatures of the woods. The sentries were ever on alert for signs of trouble, especially as rumours of the Darklings' raids escalated.

Studying the riders, Calib thought that they looked like men-at-arms rather than true knights. Still, to have an arrival for once . . . That *was* news.

Bringing up the rear of the group was a boy riding on a smaller pony. The lad had large ears that poked out from his white blond hair. He was dressed in a freshly pressed page's uniform, and his jaw was set in a tight frown. Calib wasn't very good at estimating human ages, but he thought the boy looked somewhere around ten or twelve.

'Cheer up!' said one of the men as he grabbed the boy's reins and tugged the pony towards the stables. Calib ducked to avoid being seen on the trough. 'We're at your new home! Isn't it grand?'

The boy only scowled.

Calib waited until the Two-Leggers disappeared into the stables before he climbed down and scampered across the remaining distance to the tapestry hall. Squeezing under the heavy wooden doors of the Two-Legger chapel, he entered the nave. Calib felt a familiar awe wash over him. Coloured light shone like daggers through the stained-glass windows, and the wooden pews seemed to give off a warm glow. The air smelled of aged wood and dust.

Working his way up onto the rafters, Calib emerged on a stone ledge that circled the base of the chapel's dome. The morning sun illuminated tapestries – no larger than a Two-Legger's palm – that hung just out of sight from the Two-Leggers below. The hallowed history of Camelot's mice was preserved in every stitch. Suits of mouse-sized armour stood at attention between each tapestry, like ghostly guardians.

Calib quickly set to work, fetching a carpet beater made of twigs from the corner. He beat the tapestries in a steady rhythm, studying them as he went: the grand wedding feasts, stern knights, and glorious battles. Several scenes depicted the Great War between Camelot and the Darklings.

Calib paused as he reached the last tapestry. It

showed a solemn-faced warrior, whiskers trimmed to perfection, dressed in a magnificent, wine-coloured cloak and gold armour. His eyes flashed with confidence as he brandished a broadsword high into the air. His tawny fur, and whisker pattern, were a mirror image of Calib's, right down to the small round patch of white fur on his right ear.

'Sir Trenton Christopher, felled at the Battle at Rickonback River,' read the fine silk stitching beneath the portrait. Beside the warrior stood a lady dressed in a regal purple dress. She held a mouse-sized needle and thread elegantly in her paw.

A small tingle rolled down Calib's spine. His mother had truly been the most talented seamstress Camelot had ever known. This tapestry was the last one Lady Clara had sewn before she passed away from sea fever many years ago. It had been her hope that Calib would not forget what his parents looked like.

'Hi, Mum,' Calib whispered. Sometimes Calib would talk to the tapestry as if his parents could hear him through it. Even though he knew it was silly, pretending made him feel less alone.

Calib finished his dusting and moved on to

polishing the suits of armour. By now, his cheek was throbbing. He peered at his reflection in a burnished steel breastplate. The bruise from the acorn was quickly purpling under his fur and turning into a nasty blotch. To add insult to injury, he'd also slept on his whiskers wrong and they were all askew.

He tried to smooth the ends down, but after a few unsuccessful attempts, Calib gave up. Frustrated, he looked up at Sir Trenton's kind face.

'How am I supposed to fight a real enemy if I can't even win a battle against my own whiskers?'

'A bit of oil will smooth any crinkle out.'

Startled, Calib turned and saw Commander Yvers approaching. The stout, barrel-chested mouse walked with a slight limp, an injury from the Great War. His golden fur was tinged at the ends with silvery grey hairs. He wore a simple brown robe, the kind he donned for when he did not want to be noticed.

'But something tells me that is not what is truly troubling you.'

'It's nothing, Grandfather. I was just polishing,' Calib said quickly.

Commander Yvers's kind brown eyes searched Calib's own. 'You are a mouse of Camelot, Calib.

You do not have to bear your burdens alone. "Together in paw and tail, lest divided we fall and fail," remember?'

Every mouse of Camelot knew that motto by heart. It was even inscribed on the doors of the Goldenwood Hall. Calib nodded. He was never good at hiding things from his grandfather.

'My name was entered into the Harvest Tournament as a prank, but now I'm too ashamed to withdraw and too afraid to go through with it,' Calib confessed. He felt shame creep all the way into the ends of his whiskers. 'I don't know how I'll ever live up to the Christopher name.'

Commander Yvers smiled as he looked at the tapestry of his son on the wall. 'You know,' he remarked, 'when I was a page, they used to call me Yvers Faintheart – I was so shy! Once, I even set the commander's cloak on fire with a poorly placed candle but was too scared to tell him until his fur began to singe.'

Calib couldn't imagine his grandfather as a page, much less one who would make a mistake like that. *Really?'*

'Really. And your father was worse. He tried to hide in a burdock bush to avoid his Harvest Tournament. We were removing burrs from his fur for a week! He faced the strength challenge looking like a hedgehog!'

Calib laughed, and his grandfather placed a paw on Calib's shoulder. Together, they looked at Sir Trenton's tapestry in silence.

'You know, the knights discuss the tournament candidates at length before we approve the list,' Commander Yvers said quietly. 'If you made the cut this year, it's because we thought you were ready, regardless of whether or not it was a prank.'

Calib was stunned. 'Then why am I so scared?' he asked.

'Being brave is not about lacking fear,' Commander Yvers said. 'If you are never scared, you will never understand what it means to be brave.'

Calib pondered this in silence. He was still scared, but knowing that Commander Yvers and the rest of the knights believed in him made him feel like he might have a chance in the Harvest Tournament after all.

'Camelot needs protection now more than ever, Calib. There is said to be trouble stirring in the east. And we all must be ready to defend our home. Now, if you'll excuse me, I believe I'm late to a meeting with the bell tower larks. Living so close to the sundial has made them extremely punctual.'

Calib hopped up to his footpaws and gave Commander Yvers a sharp salute with his tail. Suddenly, he felt fizzy with a sense of purpose and possibility.

Every knight, Calib thought, had to start somewhere. All Calib needed was one chance to prove himself. One chance to show that he too was a Christopher mouse: brave, strong, and wise.

Chapter Three

Again and again, Galahad remembered the last thing his mother had said to him before he left the only home he'd ever known.

'When you get to Camelot, remember to be polite and respectful to everyone, be they knights or the lowest servants.'

His mother's fingers had snagged on a knot in Galahad's hair, and she untangled it gently. Her own dark braids were tucked away under a white wimple that cascaded down her back.

'Act like you belong there, and you will.'

'But I belong *here*,' Galahad had said, trying to

quell the tremble in his voice, 'with you and the sisters.'

Lady Elaine looked her son in the eyes. 'You are Sir Lancelot's son. You belong at Camelot.'

She kissed him good-bye on the forehead and then turned him to face the two men who had come for him. They were Sir Lancelot's men-at-arms, who'd sworn allegiance to the greatest knight the land had ever known – and the father Galahad had never met. Lancelot was so busy adventuring, he couldn't even come in person to fetch his only son.

'Act like you belong. Act like you belong.' Galahad now chanted this as he threw open the doors to the dining hall. They had arrived late to the castle, and the rest of the pages and squires were already seated for breakfast. Long tables lined the hall on both sides. Trenches of grey-looking porridge were emptying faster than Galahad could blink. The space echoed with laughter and conversation.

The chatter quickly quieted, however, as all heads turned to face Galahad. He turned around and realised with a sinking feeling that Lancelot's two men-at-arms had followed him into the dining hall.

'Attention, young sires!' one of them called. This

one had chattered nonstop during the journey. He had wanted to make very clear to Galahad how lucky he was. Galahad had heard at least four times how they'd pulled many strings to get the training master to take on Galahad at his age. Most pages started at the age of nine, and he was already eleven. But with so many knights gone from Camelot recently, the castle was undermanned, and Sir Kay finally made an exception.

'This is Galahad, son of Sir Lancelot! He joins us from St Anne's Nunnery. I trust that you all will give him a warm welcome! And –' he turned to Galahad – 'I hope you show these pages a thing or two about proper manners.'

There was a stunned silence followed by low snickers. A few muttered half-hearted hellos.

'There, properly introduced,' the man said, smiling broadly. He clapped Galahad on the back and then turned to leave the hall. 'Don't forget. We expect great things from Lancelot's son.'

Mortified, Galahad slowly made his way towards the nearest table, his ears and cheeks burning hot. So much for acting like he belonged.

One of the last open spots in the dining hall was next to a boy with a single eyebrow that extended across his forehead. But as Galahad moved to sit down, the boy slapped his palm down on the bench.

'This seat's taken,' he said. 'I don't care *who* your father is.'

Galahad looked around, but there was no room to sit anywhere, since each of the pages spread out along the benches.

Keeping his head high, Galahad reached the end of the hall with the double doors. He would either have to go back and face everyone again or skip breakfast entirely.

'Did you see his face?' someone whispered. 'Looked like he wanted to run back under his mother's skirts!'

Galahad decided maybe he wasn't that hungry after all. He all but ran through the doorway.

Chapter Four

What little bravery his grandfather had inspired that morning had evaporated by the time Calib put on the armour Sir Alric had assigned him. He scurried into line behind Devrin and strapped his breastplate over his tunic. Since he was a bit smaller than most mice who faced the Harvest Tournament, it had taken a while to find chain mail that would fit him. And now he was late, with only a dented helmet, a wooden sword, and a too-large breastplate to show for it. Doubt crept back into Calib's heart like a poisonous black spider.

The paw traffic in the tunnel grew thicker as he

approached the arched doors of the Goldenwood Hall. Calib dodged through the crowds of mice, larks, and other castle inhabitants streaming through the passages. Fur crushed up against fur, and whiskers tickled Calib's face. Making a beeline for the staging room, Calib ran headlong into Sir Percival Vole.

'Careful, mousling!' The portly brown vole popped a candied seed into his mouth, and smiled. Calib tried not to make a face. Sir Percival's teeth were black with rot. The water vole was famous for loving sweets. 'You don't want to injure the only trained healer right before the tourney!'

'Apologies, s-sir!' Calib stammered as he scooted past. He made sure to keep a good six inches between him and Sir Percival's rotten-egg breath.

Calib stepped inside a long hall with rounded ceilings, and benches on the left and right sides. Every mouse-knight in Camelot's history had once taken this same path to face their Harvest Tournament challenges. He spotted Devrin and Warren standing by the doors to the arena. He scurried into line behind Devrin.

'Thought we'd have to march in without you,' she said, fiddling with her tailguard. She looked irritated. The guard did not fully cover her long tail. Warren's armour, on the other hand, shone like polished silver and fit him like a glove.

Calib opened his mouth to respond when a reedy voice sounded out.

'Greetings, contestants!'

Sir Alric skittered into the room. As Camelot's premiere engineer and metalsmith, the white mouse had designed contraptions that many credited as instrumental in defeating the Darkling forces. He was also responsible for designing the Harvest Tournament challenges.

'I just wanted to assure you three, I haven't had a page die in one my challenges yet,' Sir Alric said, blinking his pink eyes rapidly. Calib's stomach dropped another few inches. 'A few injuries here or there, yes. But all have survived! Just make sure to keep your armour on at all times.'

No, Calib wanted to say. *I've changed my mind.* But it was too late. The arena musicians trumpeted a bright tune. Already, Warren and Devrin were shuffling forward.

Calib's heart pounded as he clanked clumsily behind Devrin. He tried to step in time to the music but was too nervous to follow its rhythm.

A riot of noise and colour greeted him. Calib couldn't help admiring the Goldenwood Hall for the hundredth time. Quarried underneath King Arthur's own throne room, the stone hall served as the highest court and tournament arena for Camelot's allied creatures. The black-iron ceiling beams curved together high above his head like a bear's rib cage. Tall wooden grandstands lined both sides of the arena. They curved like parentheses, ending on the opposite sides of a raised stage.

In the centre of the stage stood the Goldenwood Throne – in truth, a broken wooden goblet rumoured to have been discarded by Merlin. The bowl of the cup was cracked open, one side missing entirely. Velvet pillows lined the inside so that a mouse could sit comfortably. Tonight, the throne glistened in the firelight.

All of Camelot's allied creatures were present this evening, from the larks who lived in the bell tower to the moat otters, from the red squirrels who lived in the orchard trees to the moles who burrowed under the gardens.

Calib scanned the stands and noticed Cecily waving her pennant at him.

'*Bon chance*, Calib!' she shouted, her voice barely audible above the din.

Distracted, Calib accidentally trod on Devrin's

tail. She gave him a withering look over her shoulder. 'Step to the beat, Cal. Ever heard of it?'

Warren snickered.

The march halted before the stage. The three pages turned to face the arena. Calib surveyed the oval-shaped pit before him, barricaded on the longer sides by the crowded stands. He thought about dashing across the dirt-packed floor and fleeing past the doors from which he'd just come. But that would be as good as admitting he would never be a knight.

From her chair next to the throne, Sir Kensington Knaps stepped forward to address the crowd.

A fearsome knight, Sir Kensington was Commander Yvers's second-in-command. It was rumoured that she had single-handedly defeated an entire battalion of rats in the Great War. With a pointed nose and crosshatched scars along her face, Kensington now looked more wolf than mouse.

'All quiet in the Goldenwood Hall!' Her voice pierced through the noise like a finely pointed needle. She fixed those who dared ignore her command with an icy glare until they quieted. 'All rise for Commander Yvers Christopher the Valiant, Darkslayer, and Master Knight of Camelot!'

The crowd stood and applauded as Calib's grandfather emerged from behind the curtain. He was dressed in wine-coloured robes – the Christopher family colour. With his golden fur brushed back like a lion's mane, Commander Yvers seemed so fearsome that Calib felt insignificant just looking at him.

'Lords and ladies, my bannermice and my people, this autumn marks the tenth year of peace and plenty among the creatures of Camelot,' Commander Yvers began. Atop his head was a silver crown that had once been a ring of Queen Guinevere's. 'It is truly a time of celebration.'

He waved his arms to calm the resounding cheers that followed. His eyes became grave and resolute.

'However, we must never let peace lull us into carelessness. It took the sacrifices of many warriors to shepherd us to safety. We owe it to them, and to ourselves, to preserve what they fought for. We must uphold the sacred oath made to Merlin, even at the cost of our lives.'

Generations ago, the mice of the castle had made a promise to the wizard Merlin. In return for Camelot's shelter and bounty, they were to protect the castle. (Two-Leggers were too unobservant and slow to notice that their pantries were being raided).

Calib felt his grandfather's gaze fall briefly on

him. He shivered. How could he ever be brave enough?

'The true purpose of the Harvest Tournament is to find those worthy of protecting the realm. In our three challenges this evening, we shall test our pages for bravery, strength, and wisdom. Those who rise above their fears this day will find themselves in the pawsteps of our mightiest warriors. Tonight, we will begin with the challenge for bravery.'

The hall was filled with murmurs of excitement. A team of five apprentices wheeled a contraption the size of three Two-Legger dinner plates into the arena. A gasp rose up from the stands. Calib felt as if his legs had been replaced by pudding.

Before them stood the most terrifying mousetrap he had ever seen. A small chunk of cheddar cheese sat in the centre of a spring-loaded wooden platform. The platform was encircled by three rows of serrated metal teeth, like the maw of a giant sea lamprey. The sharp edges looked deadlier than any of the knives in the Two-Legger kitchen.

'Each page must remove the cheese from the platform successfully. Once the cheese is removed, the trap is triggered. In order to proceed to the next challenge, he or she must jump out of danger before the blades close,' Commander Yvers said.

Devrin gave a long, low whistle. Warren's ears began to twitch.

'And so, my sons and daughters of Camelot,' Yvers said, 'let the first test begin!'

Chapter Five

'Devrin Savortooth, please step forward!'

Calib tried to cheer along with the rest of the spectators as Sir Kensington motioned for Devrin to step up, but his mouth was too dry.

Devrin raised her wooden sword in salute to Commander Yvers. Then she turned and marched towards the trap, her eyes narrowed in concentration. Calib could see the slight quiver of her whiskers betraying her nervousness.

As she approached the trap's outer ring, the audience quieted. Calib's heart quickened as Devrin placed her sword between her teeth and broke into a galloping run, charging the trap head-on. At the last moment, she released the sword into her paw. Using it as a vaulting pole, Devrin soared over the rows of sharp metal.

Calib cringed, certain that she would slice herself on the jagged edge of the innermost row. But Devrin narrowly missed the blades and landed safely. The onlookers burst into cheers. Devrin took a quick moment to wave at the audience.

Everyone waited with bated breath to see what she would do next. Calib squinted, too afraid to watch but too embarrassed to cover his eyes entirely. After a few seconds of contemplation, Devrin grabbed her own tail and tied it into a loose lasso.

She swung her tail gently back and forth, calculating its weight. Then, with a nimble toss, Devrin looped her tail around the cheese and yanked it off the platform.

With a terrific clang, the metal teeth snapped shut like a jaw. The crowd shrieked. For a few precious seconds, Calib couldn't look, certain he would see Devrin severed in two. But when the dust cleared from the arena, he saw that she had curled into a ball. The rows of teeth had closed shut only a few whiskers' length above her. The tip of her tail was bloody – but it held the cheese tightly.

Calib felt the wind rush out of him as the crowd broke into a triumphant frenzy – horns blared, pennants fluttered wildly, and hats flew high into the air. Two mice ran out to Devrin with a canvas stretcher and bandages. Shakily, she eased herself onto the stretcher and cradled her tail. She was carried to the champions' circle below the pages' section of the stands. As she passed the other contenders, she gave Calib a big wink and took a bite out of the cheese.

'Peesh ohf cake,' she said with a full mouth. 'Er, rather, peesch ohf Swissh!'

Commander Yvers stood up from the throne to speak, his eyes shining with pride.

'Devrin Savortooth, you have shown valour like the knights who came before you,' he said. 'For successfully passing the first test, Sir Kensington will present you with the Blue Badge of Bravery!'

Sir Kensington walked down from the stage to Devrin's stretcher, and pinned a blue silk ribbon on one shoulder of her breastplate.

The crowd finally quieted, and Sir Alric's apprentices reset the trap.

Merlin, if you're still out there, please find a way

to stop this tournament, Calib prayed silently to the legendary wizard.

'And the next challenger will be . . . Warren Clipping!'

Warren sauntered up to the trap, waving to the stands. Circling the outer ring, the grey mouse stopped at the hinge that linked the rows of metal teeth. He did a few muscle flexes and lunges, making a great show of stretching out his legs.

'Come on,' Calib muttered, even as a few mice tittered in the audience.

Finally, Warren climbed on top of the hinge. He licked his paw and tested the air, as if gauging the wind.

From his tunic pocket, he removed a candied cherry. With deft aim, Warren threw the cherry at the cheese, knocking it off the platform. When the trap clapped shut, Warren leaped easily off the hinge and out of the trap's way. Danger avoided, he walked to the centre and retrieved the cheese from the ground. Dusting the dirt off, Warren held it up like a trophy. The crowd went wild.

'Very resourceful, Warren,' Commander Yvers remarked. 'There is more than one way to clear a trap, and courage goes hand-in-hand with cleverness.

Sir Percival will present you with the Blue Badge of Bravery.'

Warren bowed smugly and took his place next to Devrin in the champions' circle on the far side of the arena. Sir Percival came down from the stage and pinned the ribbon. He patted Warren encouragingly on his shoulder.

'Calib Christopher, please approach the arena!'

Panic poured over Calib's head like ice water. His paws were slick with sweat. His nose had gone numb. He could barely feel his body.

'Calib Christopher,' Commander Yvers repeated. Was it Calib's imagination or had his grandfather frowned? 'Approach!'

Trembling, Calib stepped jerkily down from the platform, his head pounding as hard as his heart. The sea of cheering spectators only made him feel more like an impostor. He knew he would not succeed in getting the cheese from the trap. He would likely not make it past the first ring of metal teeth. He was not bold like Devrin; not cunning like Warren. He looked back at his grandfather. The warmth and encouragement coming from Commander Yvers's gaze was the worst of all.

Calib knew he would have to drop out of the

tournament. He wasn't ready. He didn't have the courage. He *wasn't* brave.

He was a poor excuse for a Christopher.

As Calib opened his mouth to withdraw himself, a gust of wind blew through the Goldenwood Hall. All the torches extinguished at once, plunging the hall into darkness.

For a few seconds, everyone was silent. Then the yelling, coughing, and shoving began.

'What's just happened?'

'That was a magicked wind if I ever felt one!'

'Is this some beast's idea of a joke?'

Calib could not believe his luck – his prayer had been answered! The tournament could not go on without light!

His eyes adjusting to the surrounding darkness, Calib could just make out the patchy silhouettes of his fellow mice grasping in the dark. He wiped his brow and let out a shaky laugh. He had time now – to plan, to think of an excuse.

'Friar Burrows, my tail! Ow!'

'Someone get Sir Alric up here!'

Then, out of the corner of his eye, Calib spied a skulking shadow emerging from behind the stands. Tall and lithe, it bounded swiftly towards the stage on four paws.

43

The silhouette of a curved blade sat between its teeth, and a sudden terror slammed like a crushing weight against Calib's chest. As the shadow came closer to the stage, Calib shouted.

'Guards! Grandfather! *Look out!*'

But his cries were drowned out by the confusion of other voices. Smoke caught in Calib's lungs. He pushed towards the stage, still shouting, but the shuffling and shoving blocked his way. He was buffeted in all directions, like a leaf in a swirling current of water.

'Guards! Grandfather! Look – *Oof.*'

Calib tripped over a hedgehog's drum and fell on his chin. He watched helplessly as the shadow leaped onto the stage, nimble as an acrobat. With unnatural speed, it crouched and pounced on Commander Yvers. His grandfather's silhouette twisted in pain.

'*Grandfather!*' Calib cried out.

'I've got a torch!' someone shouted in the distance, and a torch reignited in a far corner of the arena. Faint, wavering light trickled back into the hall.

Now, torches were springing up, like fireflies in the dark. At last the light made its way to the stage, illuminating Commander Yvers as he fell to his knees. A dark, wet stain blossomed beneath his fur.

Chapter Six

No. The word was like a drumbeat in Calib's chest. *No, no, no, no, no.*

Fearful voices shouted in the half-dark. 'We're being attacked!' they cried. The Goldenwood Hall was chaos as animals rushed the exits, squashing fur and paws, whiskers and ears, trying to find a way out. But Calib could think only of his grandfather. He shoved against the tide of fur, sailing on the single drumbeat, *no.* Time moved in quick bursts.

Sir Kensington was holding Commander Yvers now, cradling his head.

'We need a healer!' she barked. 'Percival! Get over here!'

Finally, Calib was there, at his grandfather's side. He grabbed Commander Yvers's outstretched paws as Sir Kensington laid him on his back. Massive clawed paw prints led a bloody trail away from his grandfather. Calib couldn't stand to look at them. Dimly, he registered that Sir Owen and three other knights had taken off in pursuit of the assassin.

'My grandson,' Commander Yvers gasped, each breath wheezing out like a punctured forge bellows. His blood pooled on the golden embroidery of his cloak. 'There's so much left to say . . . to teach . . .'

'Please hold on, there's still time,' Calib implored. He could see Sir Percival running towards them, gripping a medical bag between his teeth.

'There is never enough time. You are the last Christopher, Calib. You must carry on our legacy. Promise me . . . you will see to . . . protect . . .' Commander Yvers was no longer looking at Calib. His gaze lost focus, and his body stiffened. With a shuddering sigh, Commander Yvers closed his eyes and lay still.

Calib clutched his grandfather's limp paws. 'Grandfather,' he said, his throat swollen and raw. 'Grandfather, stay with us.'

'Come, Calib,' Sir Kensington said, laying a paw on his shoulder, her voice thick with sorrow. 'There's nothing to be done.'

Calib spun away from her, reeling. It was his fault. All his fault. He had wished for an intervention, anything to stop the tournament. And he hadn't been quick enough to save his grandfather. He hadn't been strong enough.

Calib pushed through the crowd bursting from the Goldenwood Hall, and then he started to run. Down hallways and stairwells and twisting corridors, ignoring everything but the throb of shame inside him and the thick, awful pressure behind his eyes. He ran until he thought his lungs might explode from the effort.

Blinded by tears, hardly paying attention to where he was going, Calib charged out of the mousehole he thought would lead outside the castle. Instead, he found himself on the open marble floor of King Arthur's throne room. In his misery, he'd made a wrong turn, but he knew there was a shortcut at the other end. He was halfway across the room when he heard someone cough.

He froze.

Sitting at the Round Table in front of him was

the Two-Legger boy from earlier that morning, the one with big ears.

And he was staring directly at Calib.

Calib was so stunned – he'd been seen *by a Two-Legger* – that for a second, his legs stopped working and he couldn't retreat.

'You seem to be in a rush,' the boy said in a friendly tone.

Calib wondered if this was all part of a terrible nightmare. There was no other explanation . . . unless the Two-Legger was actually *speaking* to Calib.

'I had a pet mouse just like you back at home,' the boy continued. He put down the quill he had been writing with and squatted to the ground. To Calib's shock, the boy extended a hand, as if to invite Calib onto his palm.

Alarms blared in Calib's head. Being seen by a Two-Legger equalled certain death. He darted around the other side of the table and behind the throne. From there, he began scaling up the back, using the ornate filigreed carvings as pawholds.

'Wait!' said the boy. 'I'm not going to hurt you.'

But Calib wasn't listening. He jumped onto the nearby sill of a tall stained-glass window. Spying a small missing pane in the glass, Calib squeezed through the opening. Suddenly, he was falling through the night air outside.

He landed hard on a wilting lilac bush. Winded, Calib looked around him. He was in the queen's private courtyard – a beautiful overgrown garden on the cliffside. King Arthur had built this sanctuary for Guinevere, to keep her happy while he went off on battle campaigns. From what little Calib knew of the queen, it hadn't worked.

Calib navigated the garden, still panting, still bewildered by what had just occurred. Had the boy really spoken to him? Two-Leggers, he knew, cared nothing for mice, unless it was to snap their heads in traps. They couldn't even communicate with other species, like most animals could.

And his grandfather . . . Was it possible? Was Commander Yvers really . . . ?

The tournament, the shadows, the feel of his grandfather's paw in his . . .

Calib skirted around a pond choked with green algae, past gargoyles with moss growing thick as beards on their limbs. He climbed the stone wall that lined the edge of the cliff. The castle was perched upon a small island that divided a mighty river into two streams. Those streams emptied into the Sapphire Sea by way of two waterfalls. From this vantage point, Calib could see both the northern and southern falls plummeting into the sea.

And then it hit him, like an acorn to the chest. Dead. His grandfather was dead.

No amount of wishing or magic would undo this terrible truth. He wanted to cry, but the tears felt clogged somewhere in the back of his throat.

The moon and stars hung high over the sea, turning the water into a sparkling canvas as far as the eye could see. Calib remembered tales his mother used to tell, of ships that could sail great distances, beyond what even the Two-Legger maps had charted. Perhaps he could run away and join one. Run away – as he had done just now – only farther, never to return.

'There you are!' Devrin's sharp voice rang out from the courtyard below him, cutting through the numbing fog in Calib's heart. 'All pages need to report to the council room immediately!'

'Coming!' Calib swiped at his eyes with a paw. He couldn't let Devrin see him like this. That would make things even worse. He quickly rappelled down from the wall, using a length of ivy as a rope.

'Have they found the attacker? Do we know

51

who it was?' he asked breathlessly when he reached the bottom.

'No, the devil got away,' Devrin said with a snarl. She balled her paws into fists, and her ears flattened against her head. 'But not for long.'

They scurried towards the southernmost tower, using the gutters that ran alongside the castle walls. When they arrived at its base, they entered the tower through a large crack between two stones. The building housed the castle's weapons, which were dusty from neglect. The two mice ducked behind the handle of a large mace and entered a much smaller chamber set into the thick castle foundation.

Inside was a round table, much like the one in King Arthur's throne room, except that this one was constructed from a bronze serving platter stacked on an empty thread spool. Overturned cups surrounded the table, serving as seating for the assembled knights. A rusted chandelier made of broken Two-Legger jewellery dangled from the ceiling.

The room looked dingy in comparison to the Goldenwood Hall, but this was the true heart of Camelot. From here, the mouse-knights ruled their dominion with steady paws.

One by one, the room filled to capacity. Twenty mice were seated at the Round Table, and a handful of pages ran about, refilling their thimbles with tea. The last one to arrive was Macie, a sharp-eyed red squirrel dressed in a green camouflage tunic. She was the leader of Camelot's scouts. Calib was surprised to see Macie. She was usually deep in the woods on some mission.

When everyone was accounted for, Sir Kensington motioned for Devrin to close the door behind her. Each mouse was keenly aware that the tallest chair in the room, Commander Yvers's, sat unoccupied.

'All rise for this meeting of the Round Table,' Kensington said.

The knights rose to attention and raised their sword hilts to their foreheads, facing the direction of the empty chair.

Chapter Seven

'My fellow knights,' Sir Kensington said, 'I know we are all stunned by the loss of Commander Yvers. In the wake of this heinous deed, we must rally around our greatest strength: one another.'

Sir Kensington scanned the room, looking every knight in the eye. 'Justice shall be served, and we will carry on. Sir Owen, how goes the hunt for the killer?'

'Macie sent her scouts into the woods. We lost track of the devil once he got past the moat. Ergo Toggs and his otters swear they saw nothing suspicious on the water this evening.'

'And Sir Percival, what's your news?'

'I have not done a full examination yet.' Sir Percival Vole's voice cracked as he spoke. Sir Alric handed him a handkerchief, and the healer blew loudly into it. 'But I had a chance to take a closer look at his wounds . . .'

From his tunic, Sir Percival removed a small bundle wrapped in bloodstained linen. A collective shudder rippled through the knights. Calib bit his tongue to keep from crying out.

'I found this buried in Commander Yvers's armour.' Sir Percival held out a chipped rodent tooth. 'It seems the creature tried to bite Commander Yvers's neck first, and broke his tooth on the armour. I'm afraid I must conclude that this tooth belongs to a black squirrel.'

Macie's expression hardened, and Sir Owen growled with anger. 'I knew it. Two-Bits must be responsible for this treachery!'

Owen pounded a fist on the Round Table. 'He is the only Darkling creature who could know the castle's layout well enough to carry out such an attack! By Merlin, he probably even knows where the storerooms are! He could lead the Darklings right to our food!'

Calib's breath went out of him in a woosh.

Two-Bits was the envoy sent by the Darklings every year to renew the peace treaty signed by Commander Yvers. He wasn't due to arrive for another week. The Darklings had chosen Two-Bits because he was a cousin twice removed of the red squirrels in Camelot's orchard. The squirrels had vouched for him. Though relations with the Darklings were always strained, to accuse him of assassinating Commander Yvers was grave, indeed.

'But there are whole tribes of squirrels out there,' Sir Alric said. 'The tooth doesn't necessarily belong to a Darkling.'

'The assassin could not have gotten into the arena without knowing the ins and outs of the castle,' Sir Percival continued. 'It was Two-Bits!'

'Now, Sir Percival,' Sir Kensington said irritably. 'Do not fan the flames of fear. There is still much we do not know. This tooth could belong to any squirrel.'

'If only it were just the tooth,' Sir Percival said, shaking his head sadly. 'Warren, I believe you had something to say to the company gathered here?'

For the first time since Calib had known him, Warren looked afraid.

'Tell them what you saw, page,' Sir Percival urged.

'When the lights blew out at the Harvest

Tournament, I saw a dark shadow come onto the stage,' Warren said, twisting his paws together. 'It had a bushy tail that brushed past me. He blended in perfectly with the dark, just like a black squirrel would.'

Mutters broke out around the table, and Calib clenched his paws into fists. The black squirrels of the forest were Leftie the lynx's most dangerous warriors. They hid well in the forest's shadows and were nimble climbers, capable of scaling both the tallest of pines and high castle walls. It would make sense if the assassin were a black squirrel.

'You are absolutely sure?' asked Sir Kensington. 'You know what a serious accusation you make and what consequences there will be.'

Warren nodded, keeping his eyes on the ground.

'I told you, Kensington,' Sir Owen said, shaking his fist in the air. 'The Darkling vermin have attacked. This means war!'

'Just because they live in the woods doesn't make them vermin,' Macie interjected. 'Their ways are just different from ours.'

Macie's tail was puffing up, growing bigger with her agitation. Calib had always liked and admired Macie. But if the Darklings didn't kill his grandfather, then who did?

'The Owls of Fellwater Swamps have been in flight for more than a month now,' Macie continued. 'They're flying during daylight, and in groups towards St Gertrude's ruins! I've told you: this is something we cannot ignore. Something bigger is at stake!'

'What could be bigger than an open declaration of war?' Sir Owen waved his thimble around dangerously to punctuate his point. Tea sloshed over the side, splashing onto the table. Sir Owen's anger often got the better of him. Many remembered him being mild-mannered in his younger days. But after he saw his best friend, Sir Trenton Christopher, die at the Battle at Rickonback River, he'd become quick to want to strike first.

'I bet the last whisker on my snout that the Darklings assassinated Commander Yvers to nullify the treaty. I say we mount a full-out assault on those scum! An eye for an eye, a leader for a leader!'

The conversation fractured into individual arguments as the knights began yelling at one another all at once. Calib tried to focus on what they were saying, but one thought kept pushing everything else out: he would never see Grandfather again.

Finally, Sir Kensington slammed Sir Owen's fighting staff on the table like a gavel.

'ENOUGH!' she roared. 'Commander Yvers would be ashamed of us, yammering like a bunch of squawking hens.'

A shameful silence filled the air.

'Pages, please wait outside while we vote.'

Calib, Warren, Cecily, Devrin, Barnaby, and the rest of the younger mice filed out of the room glumly. Calib's stomach felt like it was full of squirming eels. Already, the world had become a confusing and angry place.

'Now what?' Cecily said impatiently. The voices from the small council room reached a fevered pitch again. 'I want to know what's going to happen.'

'Don't worry your little whiskers off,' Devrin said with a sly smile. 'I've got my own ways of keeping tabs on the council.'

'What do you mean?' Warren asked, but Devrin merely gestured with a paw for them to follow.

Calib was torn. Half of him wanted to know what was happening in the council room. Another part wanted to bury himself in cotton fluff and pretend tonight had never happened.

But his paws, as if acting on their own, followed Devrin. One by one, the pages climbed on top of a wooden chest. There in the stone wall, hidden by a dusty cobweb, was a small, round tunnel just big enough for a small mouse to crawl into.

'The Two-Leggers drilled holes into the rock to anchor hooks for their weapons,' Devrin explained. 'This one didn't take. It goes in right above the council room.'

'How long have you been spying on council meetings?' Cecily asked.

'Curiosity killed the cat but didn't say anything about the mouse,' Devrin said with a shrug. She dropped to her belly and disappeared down the tunnel, followed by Cecily and Barnaby. Calib quickly followed suit, shimmying into the tight space and trying to keep his nose away from Barnaby's thin, whiplike tail.

The pages emerged into a small chamber. Calib patted dust from his fur as Devrin moved a stone to reveal a pebble-sized hole in the ceiling directly above the Round Table. The pages piled in close together, taking turns peering through the peephole. Calib stifled a squeak of pain as Cecily accidentally stepped on his footpaw.

'Sorry,' she whispered, turning slightly and sending the hilt of her practice rapier into Calib's side.

'Oof – s'no worry,' Calib said, shuffling more to the left. 'It's fine.'

'Shh!' Warren hushed, glaring at them and gesturing to the opening, where Calib could just make out Sir Kensington's strained voice.

'All those in favour of taking an aggressive measure on the matter of Commander Yvers's death, raise your paw.'

Calib jostled his way to a better view, just in time to see Sir Owen raise his paw defiantly. About half of the other knights also did the same, including Sir Percival.

'Those in favour of taking covert measures, raise your paw,' Sir Kensington said.

Sir Alric, the engineer, raised his paw, along with the other half of the knights. The crowd began to stir.

'What's going on?' Cecily whispered, 'I can't see anything.'

'It's evenly split,' Calib began to say before Warren pushed him aside for his turn.

'As acting commander, I will break the tie,' Sir Kensington said. 'After considering both your sides, I also vote against an attack.'

'But, Kensington, you can't possibly—' Sir Owen began to protest.

'The Round Table has spoken,' Sir Kensington interrupted.

She unfurled a long scroll onto the table. Underneath the lengthy lines of script, penned by Commander Yvers himself, were two paw prints.

One belonged to Commander Yvers. Another, a much larger one, belonged to Leftie the lynx, the leader of the Darkling forces. Rumour had it that the lynx kept the tails of every foe he'd killed and used them as whips. Some believed his one good eye was actually magicked so it could see through to creatures' hearts.

Calib inhaled. He had never seen the famous treaty before, although he'd heard about it nearly every day of his life.

'The treaty still holds,' Sir Kensington said. 'Until we catch the assassin, we have no way of knowing if the Darklings are responsible. We will strengthen our defences, and when ready, we will send out spies to uncover what the Darklings may be up to. Can we all be agreed?'

A smattering of ayes sounded around the table.

'We must prepare for the worst,' Sir Kensington continued. 'And pray that war doesn't come to us.'

Chapter Eight

Galahad glanced at Sir Kay, seated in the balcony. The fat knight was nodding off in his chair, his helmet slipping low over his eyes.

Today, Galahad and his fellow pages were supposed to demonstrate their horsemanship skills to Sir Kay, in hopes of being chosen as his squire. Sir Kay was King Arthur's elder foster brother, and now, he was keeper of the castle while the king was away. Long ago, Arthur himself had been Kay's squire. Even then, people could tell he was bound for great things. In no less than a year into his training, young Arthur had pulled out the Sword in the Stone and became a knight. These days, it was still a great honour to serve Sir Kay, even if he was cranky as a goat.

'Okay, Beatrice,' Galahad sighed, patting his pony on her nose. 'Let's wake that old dog up and show him some new tricks.'

But when he went to mount the saddle, the pony shied away and shook her head, as if to say no.

Puzzled, he tried again. Beatrice backed away farther.

The pages waiting for their turn began snickering under their breaths.

'Beatrice,' Galahad pleaded quietly, 'not today.'

Galahad put his left foot firmly in the stirrup and grabbed the pommel, but as he tried to kick his right leg over, the saddle straps broke off with a snap. Galahad and saddle slid off the pony and fell straight into a puddle of mud with a squelching plop.

Laughter broke out among the pages, startling Sir Kay from his nap. Only one of the younger pages, a redheaded boy named Bors, looked sympathetic.

'Wh—what's happenin' here?' Sir Kay pulled up his helmet and then looked around.

Galahad tried to stand up before the knight saw

anything, but half his uniform was already covered in stinky brown slime.

Sir Kay squinted down at the boy and then began to laugh with the others. His large stomach jiggled in time with his guffaws.

'Send this one to the kitchen,' he said, crossing a big line through Galahad's name with a quill. 'A sorry show, indeed. Next!'

Before Galahad squelched away, he examined the broken saddle. The straps holding it together were chewed nearly all the way through. Something – something *very small* – had just ruined his chances of being Sir Kay's squire.

Chapter Nine

'These rocks won't fly at all and you know it.'
Macie Cornwall kicked over a basket of round
river pebbles. The stones spilled out at Sir Percival's
feet, and the clatter echoed in the empty Goldenwood
Hall. Calib winced.

'The rocks on this island don't make good arrowheads,' the red squirrel continued, snatching up a
half-shaped arrowhead that Calib had been carving
all morning. She thrust it under the vole's nose.
'They are too heavy and hard. We need clamshells
from the beach.'

Sir Percival shrugged as he popped another

candied seed into his mouth. 'I'm afraid these are the best my apprentices could do, given the restrictions.'

It had been a week since Commander Yvers's funeral, one of the saddest and dreariest days in Calib's memory. The crowds had gathered on the riverbank to watch Commander Yvers's body, laid out in a varnished canoe and surrounded by flowers, disappear over the waterfall. Just as the ceremony ended, the clouds had broken, drenching everybody. It was as if, Calib thought, even heaven was weeping for the loss.

Now, Camelot was on high alert. The Harvest Tournament was postponed indefinitely. No mouse was allowed outside the borders without permission from a high-ranking knight such as Sir Percival. Sir Kensington's rules were ironclad. And Macie Cornwall wasn't the only one feeling cooped up. All week, fights and arguments had been breaking out in the halls of the castle. Tension hung thick in the air like a storm cloud.

'I'm sorry,' Sir Percival said, his voice petal smooth and sounding not very sorry at all. 'Only expeditions of a *critical* nature are approved. And these rocks look perfectly serviceable to me.'

Macie marched up to Sir Percival and stood

toe-to-toe with him. Her bushy tail unfurled to its full length.

'We're working with dried reeds for the shafts and donated feathers from the bell tower larks for the fletching,' Macie said, and broke a reed between her fingers to illustrate. She cast the broken bits aside with disgust.

'Why, if I didn't chew the leather off the Two Legger saddles myself, we wouldn't have any arm bracers to speak of! Archers are going to be the first line of defence if there's an attack. We need arrows that actually reach the far side of the moat!'

'Careful how you talk to me, *squirrel*.' Sir Percival bared his rotted canines. 'If I were you, I would be much more mindful of the tone you take with a *knight*.' He turned and walked away.

Macie waited until Sir Percival was out of earshot before she began her tirade. 'Why, that stink-breathed, rat-whiskered piece of vermin!' she yelled, kicking the empty bucket.

'I'm sorry,' Calib said quietly. Although he tried to avoid it, his eyes were drawn as though by magnetic force back to the stage, where Commander Yvers had fallen. Even though Sir Percival had the area mopped up immediately, Calib was still haunted by visions of the pool of blood and the giant paw prints that had led away from the scene.

Macie sighed and patted Calib distractedly on the shoulder. 'Tell you what – why don't you collect more reeds? Give me a few minutes to cool off.'

Calib nodded and left the Goldenwood Hall. He was relieved to put some distance between himself and the scene of his grandfather's assassination. Making his way towards the moat, his heart was as heavy as the stones he'd been carving all morning. While the other pages were running exciting errands, he'd been saddled with Barnaby as a partner and given the most menial tasks. It was as if the other mice knew how he had failed and wanted to punish him for it.

If only he could find some way to prove himself worthy of the Christopher name, Calib thought, and honour the memory of his grandfather . . .

'Hey, Calib! Wait for me!'

Calib turned to see Barnaby coming towards him. He carried two empty rucksacks in his paws. Huffing and puffing, Barnaby handed one of them to Calib.

'Sir Owen's asked us to collect crooked nails from the cobbler! Can you believe it? Our first task in town! There's a farmer's wagon in the courtyard – it could leave any minute. We need to catch it!'

An idea dawned on Calib. The cobbler's hut was in the south of town, only a league from the beach. Macie had been talking for days about their desperate need for clamshells. If Calib was quick, he could gather some to bring to her.

For the first time in a long while, Calib's spirits lifted just a little. It would mean disobeying the rules. But it would be worth it to provide the archers with the clamshells they desperately needed. He could come back a hero, at least to Macie and the archers.

After all, his own father had done plenty of dangerous missions on behalf of Camelot. Once, Sir Trenton even went to the owls and convinced them to help in the Battle at Rickonback River, the turning point in the Great War. If Calib wanted to be more like a Christopher, he would need to start taking some risks – and breaking some rules.

Less than an hour later, Calib and Barnaby were tucked under a canvas bag full of turnips, passing over the drawbridge in a farmer's wagon and heading down the southern road to town.

'And then there was the porridge and gingerbread, and a piping hot cup of cider to go with it.' For the past ten minutes, Barnaby had been regaling Calib with stories of all the treats he'd eaten in the previous week.

'Y'know, I think Ginny the kitchen mouse might be sweet on me.' Barnaby chuckled. 'Get it, *sweet*?'

'That's very interesting, Barnaby,' Calib said, although he hadn't been listening. Now that he was out of the castle, he was too nervous to make conversation. He kept telling himself that breaking the rules for a good reason wasn't really breaking the rules – but he knew the knights would feel differently if they found out what he was planning to do.

He could see the cobbler's hut coming up around the bend. He manoeuvred to the edge of the cart, clutching the railings as they bumped along the muddy dirt road.

'Get ready to jump!' Calib called over his shoulder. 'We're almost at the haystacks!'

'I hate this part,' Barnaby grumbled. He got up and positioned himself next to Calib.

The cart rolled to a stop to let some cows cross the path.

'You first!' Calib said, and took a quick step backwards to let Barnaby barrel past him.

Barnaby landed softly on the bale of hay and scampered to the ground.

'Hey!' When he saw that Calib hadn't followed, he gestured to him frantically. 'Quick! Before you miss your chance!'

'Oh, I forgot, I have to, er, m-make another stop,' Calib stuttered. 'Just go on without me, okay?'

'Wait—' Barnaby began, but by then the clatter of the wheels drowned out the rest of his protests.

Calib slumped back against a turnip, exhaling. He felt bad about abandoning his partner, but Calib knew Barnaby had no stomach for danger. To be honest, Calib wasn't sure if he did either.

The cart had reached the outskirts of town and was now picking up speed. Calib could see a sliver of the beach in the west, peeking over the next hill. Beyond that, there was nothing but the open sky.

The farmer driving the cart showed no sign of stopping, and Calib hadn't exactly thought through how he would disembark. Any faster and he'd never make the landing. If Calib was going to go, he needed to do it now, before he lost his courage – and his chance.

He eyed a nearby hillock covered in clover. With a running start, Calib leaped from the cart and flew through the air. He opened his rucksack like a parachute and tried to use it to slow his fall.

But he had miscalculated the distance! Instead of landing in the clover, he landed on the far side of the hillock, tumbling into a muddy rut and rolling down the slope before coming to a stop with a small 'oof'.

Slowly, Calib sat up, his head spinning as fast as if he had twirled on a frozen pond. He took stock of his limbs as Sir Owen had taught them to do. He wiggled his footpaws, patted his ribs, and checked for scratches. Everything seemed to be in order. Tossing his sack over his shoulder, he began his journey.

Calib could almost smell the beach air – the briny smell of salt and fish – when a peculiar tingling sensation came upon him. He slowed his running down to a trot. The air felt heavy and electrified, like the calm before a thunderstorm. As he cleared the next knoll, Calib saw why.

In front of him, illuminated by a weak ray of winter sunlight, was a Two-Legger broadsword wedged into a jagged slab of granite.

Calib blinked hard. The Sword in the Stone!

He darted over to the rock to examine it. The stone that held the sword was unmarred except for a single long fissure from which the weapon protruded. The crack ran all the way down the rock, and it looked as though someone had thrust the blade into it until it stuck.

Or perhaps the stone had once been unbroken and the incredible force of driving the sword through it had created the opening – Calib couldn't tell.

The sword was the stuff of legends, only ever appearing in Camelot's darkest hour. When it had last appeared, the Saxons invaded from across the sea, seeking greener lands since their own rocky plains couldn't grow enough food. The invaders had brought with them half-tamed weasels and stoats. These vicious beasts stripped the farmlands and nearby woodlands of vegetation so that the Britons would be weak with hunger when the Saxon armies finally attacked.

And attack they did.

The Saxons had defeated the Britons and enslaved all the Two-Leggers while they let their beasts free in the woods, terrifying both forest and castle creatures alike. Britain became a country torn apart by war and unrest, until one day, a young boy named Arthur pulled the sword free from the stone and made his claim as the rightful king of Britain.

With Merlin's help, Arthur pushed the Saxons and their weasels back across the sea and established

Camelot as his capital. Britain had lived in prosperity ever since.

Calib scrabbled onto the rock to examine the hilt of the broadsword; a large white diamond winked in the pommel. Beneath it, the sharp-edged blade gleamed like liquid moonlight. Mysterious runes were engraved on the flat of it.

Reaching out a tentative paw, Calib felt the cool metal beneath his pads. A vibrating tingle travelled up his spine, and he quickly snatched his paw back.

Old magic – perhaps the *oldest* magic – protected this sword.

Grandfather would have loved to see this.

Yvers had told him many legends of the mice of Camelot, but his favourite stories to tell had been about the *old* old days, when the world was young and still wild with magic.

Calib's whiskers twitched, and his heart beat a funny jig in his chest.

If the Sword in the Stone had appeared again, it could only mean one thing: danger was coming to Camelot and King Arthur could not save them.

Chapter Ten

Galahad studied the maps unfurled in the library. Colour-coded tokens representing coats of arms dotted the sketches of mountain ranges, seas, borders, and roads. Each one represented the location of Camelot's allies and enemies. His fellow pages shuffled around the tables for a better look.

'This evening, we're going to teach you a little something about military strategy,' Sir Kay said, addressing the gathered crowd from the centre table. 'It's up to me to make sure that you lot aren't completely clueless about where you are in the world.'

Galahad looked for his father's sigil but could

not find it. His stomach lurched with homesickness when he saw St Anne's Nunnery marked in a map covering the northern kingdoms. That life seemed so far away now.

'Behold, the world as we know it . . .'

Sir Kay gestured to the two largest maps, both showing Britain as a jagged teardrop of an island. There was a smaller island to the west marked by Celtic symbols. Everything east of the Narrow Seas was one wide, unbounded piece of land, divided up into a colourful rainbow of territories. The maps were identical except for the territories' borders.

'When our scouts adventure beyond Britain, they send back news of the changing kingdoms.' Sir Kay pointed from one map to the other. 'From one year to the next, our enemies are always on the move. It is our job to understand the threats before they are at our doorstep.'

Galahad compared the two maps. It seemed to him that many of the kingdoms had been swallowed up by a great tide of red tokens.

'What group is this?' Galahad pointed to the tokens, which bore a symbol of a white dragon against a red backing.

'Those are the Saxons, cursed be their name,' Sir Kay said. 'Why do you ask?'

'Well, it's just . . . They look like they're moving west is all,' Galahad said. 'See, if you look at these maps, they've swallowed up all these kingdoms in the past year. They're practically at the sea.'

Sir Kay chuckled and shook his head.

'That's good of you to notice, Galahad, I'll give you that. But the Saxons wouldn't dare attack Britain again,' he said. 'We ran them right off this island, with their tails tucked between their legs. They would not dare touch foot on this land while Arthur is here.'

'But Arthur *isn't* here, not right now,' Galahad corrected. 'When was the last time we sent scouts to the shore? These maps are dated two years ago. I don't—'

'Since when did washing dishes suddenly make you an expert on military strategy?' Malcolm, the page who had first denied Galahad a seat at breakfast, interrupted. Some the other pages tittered at his jibe.

'Now, now,' Sir Kay interjected, 'a knight of the Round Table is not only brave in battle, but also shows wisdom in the questions he asks. Galahad may be mistaken, but he's made a better observation today than you've had all year, Malcolm.'

Galahad cringed as Malcolm shot him a glare.

Galahad was going to pay for this later; he just knew it. But as Sir Kay droned on about the wisdom of knights, Galahad realised that his original question remained unanswered. If Sir Kay were wrong about the Saxons . . . If they did push west . . . then Camelot would be completely defenceless.

Chapter Eleven

Slowly, Calib began to climb down from the Sword in the Stone, following the fissure to the ground and landing with a slight thud. When he stood at the base of the rock, the sword was so tall that he had to tilt his head to see it.

'Why are you back?' Calib murmured.

The wind ruffled his fur, and for a second, Calib thought he heard a voice whisper back to him, scratchy and faint, like the rustling of brushes. Goosebumps raised on the back of his ears.

He had a hundred questions, but each answer, he was sure, would tell him that Camelot needed to prepare for danger. Now Calib was sure of it: they needed arrows.

Calib began to run. Darting across the meadow that separated the road from the beach, he remembered to keep a careful eye out for shadows that would mean birds circling overhead, and he stopped only when he felt cold sand underneath his paws.

The beach looked dim and desolate this late in the afternoon. The sun trickled timidly through a blanket of fog. He was farther than he'd ever been from Camelot, wandering in forbidden territory. Strong gusts of early winter wind whipped his fur back. Calib pulled his cloak's hood closer about his ears.

He hurried towards a rocky section of the beach, a steep landscape that would eventually grow to form the cliffs that protected Camelot. He knew he had to move quickly – examining the sword had taken up precious time – but the slippery rocks did not provide sure footing.

Step by step, he tiptoed along the crags, taking care not to fall into the water. Nonetheless, he was soon drenched through with sea spray.

The clams were lodged between the stony crevices, in tide pools sometimes much too deep for a mouse.

Calib squatted down and painstakingly dislodged what he could reach. He piled the shell pieces in his rucksack, like precious white truffles. Each one would eventually be whittled into an arrowhead – sharp, piercing weapons to keep Camelot's enemies at bay.

After an hour, Calib had filled only half his bag. He had been so focused on maintaining his footing, he had not noticed the sky greying. The water inched higher and higher on the rocks until a wild wave crashed and soaked him completely.

'Rat whiskers!' Calib turned to go back, only to realise that high tide had come in behind him. Much of the way was now submerged. Calib stared in disbelief, cursing his own stupidity. He was stuck on these rocks until the tide went out. The other mice would certainly notice he was missing by suppertime – if Barnaby had not told on him first.

With the sun dwindling by the minute, and Calib drenched in saltwater, the wind grew unforgiving. Calib gritted his teeth to keep them from chattering. He had never been so cold! Not even when Devrin had pranked him last winter and put snowballs in the Hurler during an early morning practice.

Calib ducked into a crevice between two big rocks to avoid the wind. He was surprised to find himself illuminated by a pale blue light. Shuffling farther between the rocks, he saw that he was standing at the mouth of a large cave leading up into the cliffside. Light poured out from inside, as if a small moon was buried underground. Calib wrapped his damp cloak across his shoulders tighter, but it offered no warmth.

Cold, wet, and miserable, Calib couldn't resist the promise of a dry place to spend the night. Praying that he would not encounter any unfriendly creatures, Calib ventured deeper into the cave.

Inside, milky-coloured tide pools spotted the cave floor. The walls were encrusted with crystal stalagmites that glowed. Calib felt as if he had happened upon an entirely new, alien world. He had never seen anything like it.

'Wow,' he whispered. Then, out of the corner of his eye, Calib spotted a blur of white.

Something was moving behind him in the darkness.

Something big.

Panicked, he spun around, backing up until he was pressed against the cave wall. A scream rose in his throat and froze there, choking him.

Near the ceiling of the cave, a stone ledge overlooked the largest tide pool.

And on it was perched an enormous white wolf.

Chapter Twelve

The wolf's stare pinned him to the spot. Its eyes were mismatched and unsettling, one icy blue, the other sea green. Calib felt as if his whole body had been replaced by soft cheese.

'Greetings, master mouse,' the wolf said at last, in a conversational tone. 'It's been a long time since I've had a visitor.'

Calib could not make his voice work.

The wolf's smile displayed all his finely sharpened teeth. 'And you are . . . ?'

'C-Calib. Please don't eat me,' Calib managed to squeak out. He was so afraid, he could feel his heart wrapping itself around his vocal chords.

'I'm Howell,' said the wolf, ignoring the second half of Calib's statement. 'Welcome to my cave.'

'Wolves don't live in caves,' Calib blurted out, unthinking.

'I am no ordinary wolf.' Howell jumped off the ledge and landed close to Calib. The mouse leaped back in alarm. Calib shook like a newborn fawn. Howell took a long sniff. 'And *you* are no ordinary mouse.'

'Oh, yes. Yes, I am. Definitely ordinary. Nothing special at all.' *Run*. That was all Calib could think. He had to run. He would risk drowning in the ocean if it meant getting away. Calib began to reach for a shell in his rucksack, with the intent of chucking it at the wolf. If he aimed directly for one of his eyes . . .

'I disagree.' The wolf exhaled. 'You greatly resemble your father, you know.'

Calib's paw instinctively flew to the white patch of fur on his right ear. He nearly dropped the rucksack entirely.

'You – you knew my father?' Calib stammered, his fear eclipsed by curiosity.

'Only a Christopher mouse could have ventured so far on his own.' Howell smiled again. This time, his teeth did not seem so scary. 'Sir Trenton did me a great service once. One that cost him much in return. I have not forgotten that. How fares Camelot these days?'

Calib, still struck with wonder, found himself slowly relaxing. He shook his head. 'Terrible things have happened . . . and the Sword in the Stone has reappeared!'

Howell frowned and tilted his great head. 'Tell me more.'

Without knowing exactly why, Calib felt like he could trust the wolf. Now that he had found his voice again, he couldn't stop the words from bubbling out. Calib recounted everything that had happened in the Goldenwood Hall that one awful night, though he left out the part where he had prayed for the tournament to be cancelled. Calib still couldn't bring himself to talk about his cowardice.

'Commander Yvers dead and Two-Bits accused?' Howell sounded troubled. 'And who has brought the charge against Two-Bits?'

'Sir Percival Vole found Two-Bits's tooth in Commander Yvers's armour, and this page – this horrible, mean page named Warren – said he saw a black squirrel. Only . . .' Calib frowned, remembering the overheard conversation in the council room. 'Only . . . I don't think he could have.'

'Assassination is not the Darkling way.' Howell swung his enormous snout from side to side, pondering this for a long moment. 'These accusations are preposterous. And how has everyone taken the news?'

'We're all preparing for another war against the Darklings,' Calib said gravely.

'War, you say?' Howell paced back and forth, more agitated than before.

'Yes.' Calib twisted the drawstrings of his cloak tightly in his paws. 'Any day now, Leftie the lynx and his hordes could ambush us again, like they did when they killed my father,' Calib continued. 'That's what everyone's saying, anyway.'

A loud growl from Howell made everything shimmer in the cave. The cave light also grew brighter, glowing a vibrant blue. Calib knew then that Howell had spoken the truth: he was no ordinary wolf. But what was he? Calib was too afraid to ask.

'Listen to me closely, young master,' Howell said. 'Your father's death had nothing to do with an ambush by the Darklings. You must know your father's legacy is much greater than what even your legends have told. The world may not see the likes of him for many an age.'

'That's the problem,' Calib said bitterly. 'Everyone expects me to follow in my father's pawsteps. But they're simply too . . .' Calib trailed off. The realisation hit him all at once.

'What is it?' Howell asked.

'Too big,' Calib whispered. 'His pawsteps were *too big*.' He looked up at Howell. 'I saw those bloody paw prints on the floor the night of the Harvest Tournament. They were massive and . . . and clawed! There's no *way* those prints belonged to Two-Bits. It couldn't have been a squirrel at all . . .' Calib's heart pounded. He needed to tell Sir Kensington immediately!

'Thanks for your shelter, Master Howell. And thanks for, erm, not eating me, and everything. But I *have* to find a way back to Camelot. I'm in big trouble already!'

'Then I'll take you back the fastest way possible.' Howell dipped his nose to the ground so that Calib could climb on top of his head.

'Are you sure this is a good idea?' Calib hated to be so blunt, especially when the wolf had shown him such kindness. But he didn't think his arrival in the night, unannounced and on a giant white wolf, would be well-received by the mice of Camelot.

Howell must have known what he was thinking. 'I know a shortcut that will allow me to remain unseen,' Howell said.

'And I won't fall off?'

'Not while you are in my care, Master Calib.'

Only half convinced, Calib reluctantly climbed onto Howell's snout and made a seat for himself between the wolf's ears. He took a few deep breaths to calm himself.

Please, Merlin, let this not be as stupid as it looks, he prayed silently. He wiped the sweat off his paws and strapped the rucksack to his back.

'Now, hang on tight,' Howell instructed.

As soon as Calib gripped Howell's ears, the wolf shot out of the cave like an arrow, bounding at a breathtaking speed. Calib clutched Howell's ears for dear life, shutting his eyes tightly as the wolf leaped from rock to rock. He heard the crashing of the waves and felt sea spray gather in his fur. The air was soaked with the smell of salt and seaweed.

Eventually, Howell's movements smoothed into long, loping gallops. As soon as Calib realised he wasn't about to slip off, he dared to open his eyes. The waves crested right at Howell's paws, and he splashed through them. The night sky above was cloudless and speckled with stars.

Howell tilted his head back slightly and howled at the waning moon.

'Aroooooooo!'

Calib felt as if the moon was howling back. A sense of triumph flooded him. He felt more alive than ever. For once, he felt invincible. If only Warren could see him now. Or better yet, if only his father and grandfather could see him riding on Howell. Feeling braver than ever, Calib joined Howell in a triumphant holler into the night.

'Awwwoooooooooo!'

Chapter Thirteen

The pair arrived at the mouth of another beach cave, this one hidden underneath a large flat rock. The opening was much smaller than Howell's – just large enough for the wolf to pass through.

'Mind your ears, young master,' Howell said as they travelled up the gently inclined tunnel.

'Where are we?' Calib asked, sliding down to Howell's shoulders to avoid bumping his head against the ceiling.

'These caves extend farther inland than you would expect. And this particular tunnel will lead you right beneath the castle,' the wolf replied.

'You know your way around the cellars, I suspect.'

'Yes,' Calib said, 'but I've never seen a way to get in or out of them except for the stairs.'

'Ah, and I doubt anyone has ever looked,' Howell said. 'This path was laid by someone who took great pains to keep it hidden. Unless you know what you are looking for, its entrance will remain concealed.'

'Who was this person?' Calib asked.

'A foolish old man who can no longer walk the earth,' Howell said. He seemed eager to change the subject. 'But tell me, how was the harvest this year?'

The wolf asked many more questions about Camelot. Calib answered as best as he could. After some time, they arrived at what looked like a solid stone wall.

Howell listened intently for a few seconds before pushing the flagstone loose with his front paws. As they squeezed through to the other side, Calib saw that they were in the wine cellar.

'How can I ever thank you?' Calib whispered as he slid off Howell's nose and onto the dirt-packed ground.

'By seeking the truth behind your grandfather's death,' Howell said. 'Somebody is weaving lies, for another war with the Darklings will bring only pain, death, and no justice.' His extraordinary eyes seemed to be flooded with secret meaning. 'It *will* take much courage to ask the right questions.'

Calib looked down at his paws.

'I'm wrong for this quest. I'm not very courageous at all.'

'I would think differently of a mouse who has just ridden a wolf,' Howell said, smiling. 'There can be great power even in the smallest warriors.'

Calib looked up to protest, but the wolf had disappeared, slipping away silently into the darkness. No ordinary wolf indeed.

Calib scampered along the base of the cellar wall to the nearest set of stairs that would lead back into the Two-Legger kitchen. By now, the mice would have finished their suppers, and everyone would have known he was missing. But Calib wasn't concerned. Once he told them where he had been, and what he had discovered, they would understand. He picked up his pace.

The kitchen looked empty. Calib sniffed the air, stepping cautiously inside. Suddenly, a paw reached out of the shadows and grabbed the back of Calib's hood.

'Well, well, if it isn't the deserter,' Warren drawled. 'I pegged you as a turncoat, but I guess you're just dumber than you look.'

He set Calib down and gave him a little shove. 'We better report to the council room this instant. Macie sent scouts out looking for you. Thought you were kidnapped by Darklings. Sir Kensington is going to flay you alive with your own tail!'

But Calib stood his ground. He crossed his arms, wishing he were at least a half inch taller.

'Funny you mention being a traitor when *you're* the one who's been lying to everyone,' Calib said.

Warren gaped at him. For a second, he said nothing.

'What are you talking about?' he finally asked.

'The assassin's tail couldn't have brushed by you. You were in the champions' circle on the other side of the arena.'

For once, Warren didn't have a good comeback. His face pinched with a shadow of worry.

'Oh yeah?' Warren shoved his nose directly into Calib's. 'If you're so sure about that, why haven't you told anyone?' Warren gave Calib a hard push, and Calib stumbled backwards. 'You're too scared, that's why! And you're going to get your hide shaved off for breaking the rules.'

But Calib had seen Warren's face and knew that his instincts were right: Warren had lied.

Warren marched Calib to the council room, where all the knights stood clustered around a large map of Camelot and its surrounding areas. Search zones were already marked on it. Barnaby sat sniffling in the corner, his arm in an improvised sling made of cheesecloth.

'Look who I found lurking around in the kitchen, hunting for a snack!' announced Warren, shoving Calib forward.

'Calib Christopher!' Sir Owen jumped up, his voice full of relief. 'Where were you off to, lad?'

'I went to the beach to bring shells for the arrowheads,' Calib said quietly. He held out the rucksack half filled with clamshells. His original quest now sounded foolish, even to his ears. Had he really believed a few broken shells would make him a hero?

'Och, I take full responsibility, sirs!' Macie came forward, waving her paws. 'Calib only wanted to get the shells as a favour to me.' She discreetly took the bag from Calib.

'I won't forget this, mate,' she whispered.

Calib's attention turned to Barnaby, who was still whimpering quietly. 'What happened?'

'The cobbler threw a shoe at me!' the mouse retorted, sticking out his bottom lip. 'Because *someone* wasn't there to be my lookout!'

Annoyance prickled Calib like a boar-bristle brush through his fur. Everyone knew Old Cobbler Hamish had bad eyes. Only Barnaby would let himself get caught in the open.

'What do you have to say for yourself, Calib?' Sir Kensington crossed her arms, waiting for an answer.

Calib thought about Warren's words and what Howell had said before he left. Calib needed to tell the truth.

'I'm sorry Barnaby got hit by a shoe, but I have very important news.' Calib sucked in a deep breath. 'Two-Bits is *innocent*. The night Commander Yvers was attacked, I saw the paw prints leading away from Grandfather. They were far too big to belong to a squirrel. They had *claws*. And Howell agreed it couldn't have been Two-Bits who murdered Commander Yvers,' he added in a rush. 'And he said the Darklings didn't murder my father.'

'Howell?' Sir Owen looked confused. 'Who is Howell?'

Too late, Calib realised he'd said too much. But now that he'd mentioned Howell, he didn't see how he could weasel out of telling the whole truth. 'He's . . . Well, you see . . . he was this wolf I met on the beach. A big white one . . .'

'You *spoke with a wolf*?' Macie's eyes nearly popped out of her head.

'He wasn't just any wolf,' Calib said quickly. 'His name is Howell, and he said he knew my father, Sir Trenton.'

'I don't care if his name was Humdinger the Fourth!' Sir Owen shouted. 'Wolves are our natural enemies! They cannot be trusted!'

Sir Percival shook his head and tsked. 'Calm yourself, Sir Owen. The poor thing is obviously hallucinating. Grief from losing his grandfather has driven him out of his mind.'

'But you don't understand,' Calib began, his voice squeaky with desperation. 'The Sword in the Stone has returned!'

A dumbfounded silence filled the room. Sir Owen found his voice first.

'Making things up won't get you out of trouble, laddie.' He tugged his one whisker and gave Calib a stern look. 'I thought I had taught you better than that!'

'But I—'

'You're a page, Calib.' Sir Kensington stepped

in. There was a cold finality to her tone that Calib dared not contradict. 'And more than that, you are a Christopher. If you can't set an example for Camelot, who will?'

Anger rose in Calib's chest. 'But I was only trying to help.'

'You abandoned one of your own, Calib. Barnaby got hit by a shoe!'

'Wasn't a house slipper, either, but a thumpin' boot!' Barnaby added.

'And were you dancing a jig two inches from his nose?' Calib shot back hotly. 'Because I don't see how else you could possibly—'

The council door suddenly swung open, slamming into the wall with a bang. One of Macie's forest scouts burst into the room. Still dressed in his leaf-coloured camouflage, the tall squirrel was breathless and panting from excitement.

'Reporting from . . . the search party, ma'am!' he gasped, saluting Macie quickly.

'We've just . . . captured . . . a Darkling crow stealing from the gardens!'

Chapter Fourteen

Calib watched open-mouthed as four squirrels marched into the council room. Together, they had a young female crow pinned between them. Her wings were restrained with a chain made from a broken Two-Legger necklace. Her pitch-black feathers were dull and indistinguishable from her threadbare cloak of the same colour.

Calib felt sorry for her, thief or not.

'My name is Valentina Stormbeak,' she said with a slight squawk in her accent. 'I'm a messenger for the Darkling nests. I take sole responsibility for my actions. I was only hoping to borrow enough food for my trip home. I'm just so hungry.'

'Quiet,' said Sir Kensington as alarmed whispers rose up from the Round Table. Macie looked devastated.

'We found this in her possession.' The scout handed Sir Kensington a torn piece of parchment. The mouse took it and read the message out loud.

'"There is strength in numbers. Join your fellow Darkling crows in a fortnight in the Slate Rocks at the foothills of the Iron Mountains . . ."' Kensington trailed off, and her face clouded over. Calib twitched his ears – the Slate Rocks were where Leftie the lynx made his lair.

Sir Owen, who had been peering over Kensington's shoulder, snatched the parchment out of her paws. He held the paper out for everyone to see. A large paw print was stamped at the bottom of it, identical to the one on the treaty.

'Leftie's paw print!' he exclaimed. 'I knew it!'

'What more evidence do we need?' shouted Sir Percival. 'They're building up an army against us!'

'What is the meaning of this, crow?' Sir Kensington demanded.

'Our stores have been raided clean. The crow clans need shelter and protection this winter,'

Valentina said, desperation in her voice. 'Leftie was only offering that and nothing else. Please, I must relay this message back to my people, or we will starve!'

'Oh yes,' Sir Owen interjected. 'I remember now. We sheltered some of your kind once. As I recall, you turned on us the minute the rest of the Darklings emerged from the woods!'

'You wanted the truth, did you not?' Valentina sounded close to tears. 'We would not seek war at a time like this, when we have had nothing to eat for days!'

'And you'll get not a crumb from us!' Sir Owen shouted, pulling his last whisker taut. 'Not until you tell us the truth about the Darkling plot!'

'There *is* no plot!' Valentina insisted. 'Where is Commander Yvers? I wish to address myself to him.'

His grandfather's name pricked Calib's heart like a bee sting.

Sir Owen crumpled Valentina's message and threw it away. 'Don't you dare speak his name. You lot know well enough where the commander is. You *murdered* him!'

Valetina's beak dropped open in surprise. 'Commander Yvers has been murdered?'

'Assassinated in cold blood during our Harvest Tournament,' Sir Kensington said, sounding a good deal calmer than Sir Owen but no less dangerous. 'I am Sir Kensington Knaps, the acting commander now.'

'Whatever bad blood lies between our kinds, Sir Kensington, I assure you, we did not have anything to do with this!' Valentina squawked. 'We Darklings are hungry, but we're not killers! We are being framed!'

Hope fluttered in Calib's stomach. Perhaps Kensington and Owen would believe his story now. He studied the bird's coal-black eyes. He didn't *think* the crow was lying.

'I will tolerate no more lies from this birdbrained murderer!' roared Sir Owen. In his fury, he drew his sword. 'The Darklings must answer for Commander Yvers!'

'You can't!' Calib shouted. Without thinking, he stepped forward, blocking Sir Owen's path to the crow. In the same instant, Sir Kensington drew her own broadsword. She blocked Sir Owen's with a clang. Calib's heart pounded as he stood still under the gleaming arch made by his teachers' swords.

'Stay your paw, Sir Owen,' Sir Kensington said between clenched teeth. Her voice was barely above a whisper, yet it seemed to chill the entire room. 'This is not what Yvers would have wanted. We will have the prisoner taken to the cellar dungeon, *with* food, and we will question her again when emotions are not so high.'

Surprised at the rebuke, Sir Owen sheathed his sword, but not before giving Valentina one last scowl.

'As you say, Kensington.' The black mouse marched to his seat and drank deeply from his flask of elderberry wine.

Sir Kensington turned to Calib, whose legs suddenly felt like wet noodles. Calib couldn't believe he had just stood up to Sir Owen – one of the most fearsome mouse-knights of Camelot.

'As for you, Calib Christopher, you are relegated to kitchen duty starting this evening. You will no longer be part of the war effort and are relieved of your page duties for the time being.'

Calib felt like someone had gutted him from the inside. 'But—'

'We all made a promise to your father a long time ago that we would look after you like one of our own babes,' Sir Kensington continued. 'This is as much for your own good as it is a punishment. You have shown that you are not ready to defend Camelot.'

Calib opened his mouth to protest.

'*No*,' Kensington said, holding up a paw before he could get another word out. 'No more excuses. We're done here. To the kitchen this instant.'

Chapter Fifteen

A pile of scattered straw lay in the wooden frame where Galahad's mattress was supposed to be. His pillows and blankets were nowhere to be found.

Galahad scanned the dormitory room for the culprits, though it was not hard to see who they were. A few pages were poorly concealing their laughter, and in the centre was their leader, Malcolm.

Exhausted after washing dinner dishes all evening, Galahad felt his last shred of patience evaporate. He marched up to Malcolm and the rest of his lackeys.

'All right, I get it. You don't like me,' Galahad said, crossing his arms. 'I don't want to be here with you, either. So just give me back my bedding, and I'll find somewhere else to sleep tonight.'

'Oh yeah, kitchen nun, what if we already chucked it into the manure pile?'

Galahad hesitated, unsure whether Malcolm was bluffing. Fighting had been forbidden at the nunnery. Would it get him in trouble here?

'What, nothing to say without Daddy around?' Malcolm taunted, edging in even closer until he was mere inches from Galahad's face.

'I've heard that his father doesn't even want him,' said one of the pages in Malcolm's cohort.

'Ha!' Malcolm's warm breath hit Galahad square on the nose. 'I bet he's ashamed. I bet he left the castle just so he wouldn't have to look at your ugly face.' Malcolm flicked Galahad's ear for good measure.

Rage shot through Galahad like a lightning bolt. Without thinking, he threw a punch that connected squarely with Malcolm's eye.

'Fiiiiiight!'

The shout brought all the pages running in from the other rooms. They circled around Malcolm and Galahad like a pack of wolves. Malcolm brought

Galahad down, and the two boys rolled onto the floor. Galahad tried to counter Malcolm's rapid-fire punches and kicks. He'd never been in a fight before, but Malcolm obviously had. The bigger boy managed to sock Galahad in the stomach, knocking the air out. Before Galahad could recover, Malcolm had him in a headlock.

'What in Merlin's name is going on here?' A gruff voice cut through the commotion. The pages rushed back to their bunks like nothing had happened. Malcolm and Galahad were still on the ground, locked in a struggle.

Sir Kay stood in the doorway with his arms crossed and his nostrils flaring. His usual boorish scowl was made somewhat less frightening by his lavender-coloured night robes.

'The new boy is picking fights!' Malcolm promptly let Galahad go. 'He says he doesn't even want to be here!'

Galahad's face felt like one giant bruise. Something warm trickled down his forehead. He reached up, and his fingers came away from his brow sticky and red with blood.

Sir Kay raised a dismissive hand. 'Save it for later – you know the rules. No fighting outside of the training arena. Malcolm, you've earned yourself extra stable duties for the next month. Galahad –' Sir Kay turned his attention on him – 'tomorrow, you will begin a new assignment as Sir Edmund's personal assistant. The rest of you pages will run extra laps tomorrow for waking me up.'

The collective groan was quickly silenced by Sir Kay's warning glare.

'Being a page of Camelot is an honour bestowed upon few. Take care to remember that, all of you.' He pivoted out of the room and slammed the door behind him.

Bruised and fuming, Galahad lay down on the pile of straw and pretended to go to sleep. He'd made his decision. He knew what he had to do.

Late into the night, when he was sure everyone around him was fast asleep, he snuck out of the dormitory with all his belongings tucked under his arm.

He would need to steal enough food to last him at least three days. The woods outside the castle were rumoured to be full of many threatening crea-tures . . . but they couldn't possibly be any worse than those he'd encountered at Camelot.

Chapter Sixteen

Calib stood alone in the kitchen, scrubbing dirty dishes in a big basin. The injustice of everything that had happened earlier in the evening still filled him with bitterness. A clean dish slipped out of his hands, dropping back into the grey water.

'Rat whiskers!' he cursed.

A small giggle made Calib turn around. Cecily was standing at the kitchen entrance.

'Come to have a good laugh?' Calib said, heat rising behind his ears. Cecily was the last mouse he wanted to run into while he had flecks of food all over his fur.

'Sorry,' Cecily said. 'I came to help, honestly. As the head cook's daughter, I've learned to do the dishes quickly so I could have more time for training.'

Cecily stood next to Calib and attacked the dishes with a ruthless efficiency. She soaped several at once, before plunging them into a pot of clean water to rinse them.

'Thanks, Ceci,' Calib said sheepishly. The chore went faster with an extra set of paws.

'I heard that you pulled quite the stunt today,' Cecily said above the clatter of plates. 'Speaking with wolves and coming to the defence of a crow!'

'And look what good it did me,' Calib grumbled, gesturing to a pile of dishes.

'Well, I want to hear it from the mouse's mouth.'

Calib recounted his adventures at the beach, including the reappearance of the Sword in the Stone, and Howell's request. 'And the tail couldn't have brushed by Warren from where he stood. He's lying, I just know it!'

Calib braced himself for ridicule, but Cecily only looked thoughtful.

'You're right,' she said slowly, as if she was picturing it for herself. 'I was sitting right behind the champions' circle. There's no way the assassin could have come by there.'

'Well, it's my word against his, so it doesn't mean much,' Calib said.

'But it does,' Cecily said. 'If Two-Bits didn't do it, then we're preparing for war against the wrong enemy.'

'But no one will believe me!' Calib said. 'And even when they do find the Sword in the Stone, Sir Owen will probably say it's *more* proof that the Darklings are planning to attack Camelot.'

'*I* believe you.' Cecily took Calib's paw in hers and squeezed it. 'Now we just have to prove it to everybody else. I think we need to make a visit to the cellar and talk to Valentina.'

'You know where she's being kept?' Calib asked.

Cecily nodded. 'Sir Kensington tasked me with delivering food to the prisoner.'

Calib gulped. Talking to the prisoner would mean more rule breaking. But he knew Cecily was right. They had to be sure they were preparing for war with the right enemy.

The two friends quickly wiped off their paws. Leaving behind a shining tower of clean dishes, they took off down the tunnels that led to the storage cellars deep underneath the castle.

There, the air felt dry and cool and smelled of salt. Cecily lit a small match to use as a torch, illuminating their immediate surroundings and casting long shadows. Enough food had been packed in these sprawling caverns to last the entire castle through the winter ahead. Bunches of dried cod hung from the ceiling like scaly chandeliers. Barrels of lard and smoke-cured meats lay stacked against the walls.

Scurrying alongside the barrels, they slipped through a large crack in the back wall that led into another room – one that even Two-Leggers avoided. Calib saw why as soon as they entered. It was where they kept King Lot's prized possessions.

When King Arthur and his knights first arrived at what was now Camelot, the land had been in control of an evil Saxon king named Lot.

An avid hunter, Lot would turn many of his kills into personal trophies. The heads of deer, bears, and wildcats lay scattered about, each of them frozen in their last deadly snarls. Calib knew they'd been some of the luckier ones. King Lot had a habit of keeping animals in cages and forcing them to fight for their survival. He and his men would organise these matches for their own amusement.

Now, stacks of the empty cages lined one wall, ranging in sizes for various animals. A shiver raised the fur on the back of Calib's neck.

Cecily pointed to one of the birdcages sitting atop a nearby table.

'That's her,' she whispered. They began climbing up the side of the cages, using the wires as pawholds. Once they reached the table, Calib saw that Valentina still had her wings pinned behind her. The crow's head was bowed nearly beak to chest.

'Hello, uh, Madame Valentina,' Calib ventured, stepping nearer to the cage.

Valentina Stormbeak swung her head around and squinted into the dark.

'Tiny fur-beasts,' she said wearily. 'Come nearer and I'll peck your beady eyes out.'

'I'm Cecily, and this is Calib,' Cecily said. 'Are you hungry? I wasn't sure what crows ate, but I brought you this.'

She took out a package of candied walnuts from her satchel and held them out with her paw. Calib was impressed by how still her paw was. The crow narrowed her eyes and then turned to look at Calib.

'I know you,' Valentina said, her voice softening. 'You are the one who tried to protect me.'

'We don't believe the Darklings killed Commander Yvers either,' Calib said. 'We need to find out who did before war breaks out.'

After a moment's pause, Valentina stretched out her neck and gobbled up the walnuts hungrily.

'Thank you,' she said in between swallows. 'I'm glad someone at Camelot can still think sensibly. We Darklings have enough to worry about with winter coming. Why would we start a war now?'

'You said that your stores had been raided,' Calib asked, remembering Howell's warning about a new evil at work. 'Do you know who took your food?'

Valentina shook her head. 'No. Not exactly. Something prowls the woods at night, stealing supplies and killing at whim. Leftie is our only hope of outlasting the winter.'

'Leftie the lynx?' Calib asked. 'But he's ruthless and cruel!'

'Haven't you ever heard that the sharpest claw protects the softest heart?' The crow shifted her pinned wings with a slight squawk. 'He is the only one capable of uniting the Darklings against whatever lurks out there.'

'Could you send a message to Leftie?' Cecily asked Valentina. 'And ask him to come and clear his name?'

'Kawkaw!' Valentina laughed. 'Why would Leftie leave the safety of the Darkling forest and put himself in danger just to prove that he didn't do the crime you're wrongly accusing him of?' she asked.

'Then maybe *we* can go to *him*,' Cecily said staunchly. 'As a show of good faith?'

'You saw how Sir Kensington punished me just for collecting shells,' Calib pointed out. 'Going to speak with Leftie in his lair would be treason *and* suicide.'

'It wouldn't be easy, mousling,' Valentina said thoughtfully. 'But it *is* possible. You just have to offer something he wants.'

'What could we possibly offer him?' Calib asked. 'A creature as fearsome as he is could take anything he wanted.'

'Not everything,' the crow replied. She ruffled her feathers. 'Leftie seeks Merlin's Crystal from the owls.'

Calib felt his heart speed up. *Merlin's Crystal.*

'What's that?' Cecily asked.

Valentina's beak opened in surprise. 'You mean this little fur-beast does not know about Merlin's treasures?'

Sometimes Calib forgot that Cecily and Madame von Mandrake had only moved to the castle just a year ago. Cecily shook her head.

'Before Merlin disappeared,' Calib said, eager to

share one of his favourite stories, 'he entrusted treasures to the three animal factions – those who live in the Darkling Woods, in Camelot Castle, and in the Fellwater Swamps. Leftie and the Darklings were given a hand mirror with which they could see the future.'

'We had used Merlin's Mirror to help us predict the seasons,' Valentina added softly. 'But the treasure was smashed in a Saxon raid not long after it was given to us. We resorted to raiding only to survive.'

'As for the owls,' Calib continued. 'General Gaius Thornfeather was given Merlin's Crystal, a gem that supposedly unlocks great strength to those who know how to wield it.'

'And what about us?' Cecily asked, sounding excited. 'What did we get?'

Calib gestured to the space around them. 'This castle,' he said. 'According to my grandfather, Merlin entrusted the protection of Camelot, his greatest treasure, to us. We call it Merlin's Promise. For as long as we mice live off Camelot's food, we must protect those who make it.'

Calib did not mention that there were some in Camelot who believed that Merlin *did* give Commander Yvers another, secret treasure. But if he had, Yvers kept it a closely guarded secret. Not even his most trusted knights nor his grandson knew for sure.

'So why does Leftie want Merlin's Crystal?' Cecily asked.

'Leftie wants to figure out how to unlock the crystal's great strength and use it against whoever has been stealing our food. We need it more than the owls now,' Valentina said. 'Something evil lurks in our woods at night. And Commander Yvers's assassination is only a piece of a larger plot against us.

'Unfortunately, the owls have refused Leftie's request to use Merlin's Crystal to fight the threat.'

Cecily nodded. 'I've heard that the Owls of Fellwater Swamps never side with anyone but themselves.'

'That's not *exactly* true,' Calib said quietly, rubbing the white fur patch on his ear. 'The owls intervened on the castle's behalf at Rickonback River.'

'After your father convinced them to,' Cecily added, also remembering.

Valentina blinked rapidly. '*You* are Sir Trenton's son?' She hopped closer to the bars of her cage to get a good look. 'But of course, I see the resemblance now. If anyone can get the owls to listen, it would be *you*!'

'My father was the *only* mouse who ever emerged alive from the owls' nest, and the stories say he had Merlin's help,' Calib protested. 'It's too risky.'

He thought of Sir Tormund the Foolhardy, who had gone to visit the owls fifty years ago and was never seen again. Only his blood-speckled copy of *Dialects of Taloned Fowl* was found. It was still on display in the library.

'But war could be declared any second,' Cecily pointed out.

'I'm afraid I can't be much more help from here,' Valentina said sadly. 'And because of my own weakness, my clan will starve.'

'Maybe there is a way for us to get you out,' Calib said, his sense of justice overcoming his apprehension. He would likely be exiled from Camelot for good if it was discovered that he'd freed the crow, but he knew that she had been wrongly imprisoned. Freeing her was the honourable thing to do.

The cage had no latch or lever and only a single, small keyhole. The key itself was likely hanging around the neck of Sir Kensington. But Calib found the cage door's spring-loaded hinges. He tried to wedge his tail into the hinges and pop out the springs.

Suddenly, Cecily grabbed his shoulder. 'I think I hear footsteps!'

'No one comes down here but the mice,' Calib began, but then he paused, for he heard it too. Loud, plodding footsteps that could only belong to one kind of beast: a Two-Legger.

Chapter Seventeen

'We have to hide!' Cecily whispered.

The thudding footsteps were coming closer, and candlelight spilled around the corner. Calib tried to run from the cage, but his tail was stuck. Sweat broke down his back.

'Now!' Cecily was practically shrieking. She grabbed Calib's tail and pulled hard. Calib bit on his tongue to stop from yelping. Finally, it slipped free. He ran with Cecily to hide inside the mouth of a stuffed bear. Calib knew the bear was long dead, but he couldn't stop worrying that at any second the mouth would clamp shut and the teeth would sever him in two.

A Two-Legger boy entered the room with a candle in one hand and an empty sack in the other. He hadn't grown into his lanky limbs yet, and his ears and nose were far too big for his face. But his eyes were an earnest-looking grey colour that struck Calib as familiar. Then he remembered – this was the same boy who'd tried to talk to him on the night of the Harvest Tournament!

'I could have sworn this led to the food stores,' the boy muttered. He began to rummage through the items strewn about the room. He moved quietly for a Two-Legger. Calib wondered if he was sneaking around too.

The boy turned his attention to the cages and began peering inside them. Calib shrank farther into the shadows and watched as Cecily did the same. Valentina froze in place, perhaps hoping to pass as a stuffed bird.

In one of the cages, the Two-Legger found a small hunting knife. He set off a small cascade of cobwebs and dust as he reached high and grabbed it. Some of the dust fell on Valentina's beak. The crow sneezed and lost her balance.

The boy jumped and nearly dropped his candle.

Valentina toppled over onto her side, her wings still tied up in the chains. She let out a small, defeated squawk. Calib winced, fearful of what would come next.

'Now, how did you end up in here?' the boy asked, walking over to the caged bird. He set the candle down next to the cage and examined the hinge of the door. He pulled out the small hunting knife.

Calib held his breath as he watched the knife's tip descend. But the boy wasn't aiming for the bird. Carefully, the Two-Legger used the knifepoint to push the spring that Calib had just abandoned. A second later, it bounced out with a pop!

The boy smiled and continued to work on the second hinge. The crow cocked her head to the side and watched with curiosity.

'You look like you're a long way from home,' the boy whispered to Valentina as he concentrated on wedging the knifepoint between the spring and the hinge. 'I know the feeling. Now, hang tight. I almost have it loose . . .'

The door fell open with a clang. Valentina remained still. The boy peered at the crow and then reached out his hand.

'Don't be afraid,' he said gently. 'I'm just going to untangle you, all right?'

The Two-Legger gently unwound the necklace from her wings. Once she was free, Valentina stretched out her wings to their full span and bowed graciously to the boy.

Grinning, the boy bowed back. Without warning, Valentina flew off into the next room and disappeared into the darkness.

The boy let out a soft laugh. 'I guess it's time for me to fly the coop too,' he said. 'Once I find the food, that is.'

He turned to leave the room but paused to look over his shoulder at the bear's mouth. Calib and Cecily gripped each other. After a moment that seemed to last an age, the boy shook his head.

'Must be seeing things,' he muttered, making his way back up the stairs.

As soon as he left, the two mice tumbled out of their hiding place.

'The Two-Legger did it!' Cecily said excitedly.

'Yes, but where did Valentina go?'

The two mice ran into the next room and squinted into murky darkness.

'Pssst, up here!' Valentina's head peered down

at them from a small jutting brick. 'Now, how do I get out of here?'

'I know a way,' Calib said, recalling his wild ride with Howell earlier that night.

He retraced his steps back to the loose panel in the wall. 'There's a tunnel here that leads down to the ocean.'

It took two mice and one crow pushing as hard as they could to budge the stone open a few inches. Pressing her wings close together, Valentina managed to squeeze through into the wider tunnel.

'Thanks to you, my clan will not starve this winter,' Valentina said. 'I will remember your kindness, Calib and Cecily, should you make your way to Leftie's lair. Good luck with everything!'

'Good-bye!' the two mice chorused in return, waving.

Valentina flew down the tunnel. The sound of her flapping wings faded into silence.

Chapter Eighteen

Galahad clung to the side of the tower wall like a stranded billy goat. Climbing down from the window of the squires' quarters had seemed like a good idea. But he hadn't accounted for all the extra weight in his bag. And he also hadn't expected the stones of the wall to be so tightly packed together.

After ten minutes, he still hadn't reached the ground. He tried to find a crevice for his toes and accidentally trod on the cloak he had stolen from Sir Kay. Galahad lost his footing and fell, crashing through the branches of a lilac bush on his way down. He landed hard on his back. The contents of his pack stabbed painfully into his shoulders.

'I'm afraid there's no way out of here except by the cliffs.' A woman's voice broke through the night.

Galahad rolled over and looked up at the amused face of a lady. Her dark hair hung loose past her shoulders, adorned by a simple circlet: Queen Guinevere.

Galahad stared at her, his mouth open, before remembering himself and propping himself up on one knee. 'I'm sorry, Your Majesty! I—I—was just taking in some night air when I, um, slipped.'

'I see,' Guinevere said, one eyebrow raised. 'And you felt it necessary to carry all your belongings on this night stroll?'

Bathed in pale starlight and wearing a long white cloak over her nightgown, Queen Guinevere resembled a ghost of her daylight self. The first winter snowflakes whirled past her like playful sprites. She looked at Galahad with green eyes that seemed to take in more than just his face.

'It, um, always helps to be prepared,' Galahad lied, glancing up to see if the queen was angry.

Guinevere smiled. 'Rise, Galahad, son of Sir Lancelot. And do not worry. I often have the same thoughts as you.'

'I'm not sure what you mean. I was just taking a walk—'

'And I am not so dim-witted that I don't see the castle for the cage it can be,' she said gently.

Galahad's shoulders slumped.

'I don't suppose you'll help me run away?' he ventured.

She laughed softly and shook her head. 'Come, walk with me.'

The queen motioned for Galahad to follow her. They arrived at the garden's centre, where a still pond covered in nearly frozen lily pads awaited them. Guinevere picked up a branch and pushed away some of the plants, revealing the dark water underneath.

'I found this among my things, shortly after Merlin disappeared,' Guinevere paused. 'I think he meant for us to use it.'

From the pocket of her dress, the queen removed a hand mirror. It was small, no larger than the palm of her hand. The handle and frame were adorned with iron roses and thorns. Guinevere took care to avoid the thorns as she lifted the mirror to reflect the water.

'I know that you wish to make your own way in the world, but I believe there is a higher calling for you right here. I'm afraid my talents were never as strong as Merlin's, but perhaps you will have better luck. Could you tell me what you see in the mirror?'

'Yes, Your Majesty,' Galahad said, feeling confused. He was not sure what Guinevere thought he would see.

Galahad stooped and turned to look into the mirror. At first, he saw nothing but the ripple of the moon in the pond. But after a moment, the water reflected in the mirror began to bubble and swirl, changing to a blood-red colour. Fire wreathed the inside edges of the mirror. Galahad felt nauseated, like he might fall into that abyss. Shaken, he forced his eyes away and stumbled back.

'I don't understand,' Galahad said, sitting back on a stone bench to steady himself. 'Everything turned red and fiery. What does it mean?'

'Then it is as I feared. Blood, smoke, and flame mean only one thing,' Guinevere said. Her lips were set in a grim line. 'War is coming.'

Chapter Nineteen

It felt like Calib had only just closed his eyes when a fully armoured Devrin barged into the dorm, clanging a pair of salt spoons above her head.

'Rise up, cheeseheads! Everyone is to report to Goldenwood Hall immediately! No breakfast, no lollygagging!'

Calib groaned. He had gotten almost no sleep in the night. After he and Cecily snuck back to their beds, Calib had lain awake, half expecting his role in Valentina's escape to be uncovered at any minute.

Devrin began shaking the shoe in which Warren was nestled.

'Go away!' Warren threw his pincushion pillow at her as he fell out of the shoe.

'Take it up with Sir Kensington yourself. All the knights are already at Goldenwood Hall and armoured up!'

'What for?' Barnaby grumbled. 'Are we redoing the Harvest Tournament?'

Devrin rolled her eyes. 'Fair warning, everyone, Kensington is in a foul mood this morning.' She left with a final crash of spoons.

Crankily, the pages got out of their beds. While the mice around him put on their colourful page uniforms, Calib put on a grey winter tunic instead. His demotion to kitchen mouse stung like a splash of ice water to the snout.

The Goldenwood Hall was draughty at dawn. Only a few sparse torches offered any warmth. Calib shivered as he filled everyone's thimbles with elderflower tea. The knights sat in their seats on the grand stage, shifting uncomfortably as they adjusted their armour.

Other inhabitants from the castle began to trickle in. They milled around the stage, sleepy and disoriented. Farmer Chaff, head of the field mice, was in deep conversation with Signor Molé of the garden moles. The moat otter leader, Ergo Toggs, sauntered in, followed by other representatives. Calib also recognised the guild leader for the shrew seamstresses and the porcupine carpenters.

'*Zut alors*, why have we been called at such an early hour?' Cecily's mother yawned widely.

'This was a call to arms,' a church mouse said, stroking long whiskers. 'It hasn't happened in at least ten years!'

'I don't see why we larks have to be bothered by such nonsense,' said Flit, general of the bell tower larks. 'And without a proper Feather Offering!'

'A proper what?' asked Madame von Mandrake.

'To be granted a proper audience with a bird commander, one must present them with a feather from their own kind,' the bird said a little impatiently. 'The custom applies to all birds, from the meekest sparrow to the fiercest owl.'

At the mention of owls, Calib scooted closer to listen more carefully.

'When Commander Yvers was in charge, he never forgot a feather. And we were *never* woken before dawn.'

'Precisely! The head cook needs her beauty sleep!' Madame von Mandrake said, and the conversation returned to the time of day.

Calib lightly tapped Flit's wing. 'I was just over-hearing what you said, General,' he began, trying to sound casual. 'So, in theory, if one wanted to talk to an owl leader, one would need an owl feather?'

The lark eyed him quizzically. '*In theory*, yes. If you can show them one, they will honour your right to speak with them. They should listen – but it won't stop them from eating you after you've talked.'

Calib nodded, feeling queasy. His mind knotted with the problem of getting an owl feather, never-mind the prospect of getting eaten.

Everyone hushed as Sir Kensington entered the room. Kensington's fur was washed and combed straight back, giving her a severe impression. The crosshatched scars along her snout were more noticeable than ever. Her armour, while not new, was recently oiled, and someone had hastily sewn commander stripes onto her cloak. Calib felt a hollow ache pulse in the back of his throat as he saw Commander Yvers's crown sitting atop Kensington's head.

Kensington walked to the Goldenwood Throne and sat in it for the first time. The energy in the room shifted visibly as all the knights sat up a little straighter. Calib's insides bristled. Even though he knew the throne was meant for Camelot's leader, it still felt like only Commander Yvers should sit there.

'We have not heard a call to arms in many years, Sir Kensington,' remarked Ergo Toggs.

'I'm afraid it is Commander Kensington now,' she replied. 'Last night, our guards intercepted a Darkling crow raiding our stores. They discovered a cryptic message in her pouch and brought her back here for questioning.'

Scandalised whispers rippled through the audience.

'And where is the prisoner now?' asked one of the otters.

Calib threw a quick glance at Cecily, who was standing by the main door. He saw that her dark eyes were wide, mirroring, he was sure, his own expression.

Commander Kensington drew in a sharp breath. 'Sometime in the night, the crow escaped.'

Cecily shrank back against the wall. Calib's paws began to tremble. He tried to keep his face blank as an explosion of outrage sounded from the audience.

'How?' one of the porcupines asked over the hubbub. 'How is that possible?'

'All we know is that she had assistance,'

Commander Kensington said darkly. 'Only a few of us were even aware of the crow's capture. For that reason alone, I believe there is a spy among us.'

There were renewed shouts and protests.

'I have discussed the matter with my knights,' Commander Kensington said, raising her voice to be heard. 'At this time, we have no choice but to declare open war against the Darklings.'

The hall went silent.

Shocked, Calib kept pouring Sir Percival's tea even after the cup was full. He quickly mopped up the spillage with his sleeve.

'I will lead a force to confront Leftie himself,' Commander Kensington announced, her voice brittle and hard. 'We depart at noon, after we've marshalled enough supplies for the journey.'

Calib wanted to scream. It was wrong, all wrong! If Commander Yvers were here, he would put a stop to it. But he wasn't here, and Calib had no proof to prevent the inevitable bloodshed.

The guilt was unbearable. He couldn't simply stay there, pouring tea, knowing that he and Cecily had ignited the war they had been trying to prevent.

As the knights began to discuss the details of their attack, Calib casually dumped out the rest of the tea into a nearby plant. When he returned to serve Sir Alric, he let out a squeak as though surprised to find the kettle empty.

'I guess I'll need to get back to the kitchen for more tea!' Calib said loudly, hoping he sounded convincing.

He hopped down from the stage and rushed out of Goldenwood Hall, trying to ignore the panic worming through his insides. He knew he had no hope of outpacing the seasoned soldiers, no matter how big of a lead he got. His only chance now was to convince the owls to give him Merlin's Crystal and then fly to Leftie's mountain lair.

And in order to do that, he would need to get his paws on an owl feather.

'Wait for me!'

Calib turned to see Cecily running towards him.

'You aren't going to see the owls without me, are you?' she asked breathlessly when she caught up to him.

'Wait a whisker, *we* are not going to see the owls,' Calib said, stopping in his tracks. 'I'm going alone. You're still a page. If you got in trouble, you'd lose your chance at becoming a knight! I have nothing left to lose.'

'What good is being a knight if I can't do any

good?' Cecily crossed her arms. Her neck fur bristled with annoyance. 'Scared that a girl will show you up?'

'That's not it at all!' Calib protested. His whiskers twitched irritably. 'I just don't want to worry about putting anyone else in danger. You saw what happened to Barnaby when he—'

'You're comparing me to *Barnaby*?!' Cecily was visibly angry now. Her upper lip was pulled back slightly, revealing her teeth.

'Look, I'm bad luck!' Calib said. 'I—I can't be responsible for something terrible happening to you. I can't be responsible for you, period.'

Cecily's face hardened. 'Fine,' she said coldly. 'I don't want to be a *burden*.' She spun around and bolted in the other direction.

Calib watched Cecily run away. An apology formed on his tongue, but he held it back. Better Cecily be angry *at* him than in danger *with* him.

Chapter Twenty

Time was working against Calib.

He knew he would not be able to find an owl feather simply lying around the courtyard – but he *might* be able to find one in the Two-Legger throne room. King Arthur himself signed many laws into being with the feather of a rare snowy owl. But retrieving it would not be easy. It sat smack-dab in the centre of the Round Table.

Calib broke into a run towards the throne room. Quickly climbing up into a curving tunnel with colourful panels lining one side, Calib found a loose tile and moved it aside, emerging onto the stone ledge that circled the vaulted dome of the throne room.

From this vantage point, Calib could see the Two-Leggers gathering below. They milled about a circular table carved from rose-coloured marble. Tall, high-backed wooden chairs surrounded it: the Round Table.

The table was more than just a table. It was a symbol of King Arthur's philosophy: a king should not have absolute power. True power came from many unified voices. It was the same philosophy that the mice of Camelot shared: 'Together in paw and tail, lest divided we fall and fail.'

Calib scanned the faces. Only a dwindling number of King Arthur's advisers, servants, and squires still resided in the castle. A handful of old knights sat at their places at the Round Table, their adventuring days far behind them. The quill stand sat in front of King Arthur's seat. Calib's heart sank. The stand was too visible. He had no hope of sneaking past all the assembled knights.

He spotted a boy a few feet below him, his large ears poking out from a hideous velvet hat. It was the same boy who'd rescued Valentina – the same boy who'd actually addressed Calib as though expecting him to talk back. The Two-Legger was wearing a purple server's uniform and looked bored. He held a plate full of dried dates. Every few seconds, he would slowly dip one in a large cup of sugar and hand it to frail Sir Edmund, who was seated at the Round Table.

Something white flashed in the boy's hat as he turned to pass a sugared treat. Calib's chest tightened. A barn owl feather poked out of the hat's brim.

The quill was beyond his reach, but Calib was desperate enough to make do with what he could get right now.

A blare of trumpets startled everyone in the room to attention. A tall, willowy woman strode in. She was dressed in an emerald-green dress that matched her eyes. A delicate gold crown sat high on her head, with thin braids entwining it into place. Queen Guinevere was a sight to behold.

She stood in front of King Arthur's seat at the table. The knights and advisers at the table stood and bowed, some more readily than others.

'Lord champions and knights, defenders of Camelot, thank you for meeting with me today,' she said in a clear voice that reminded Calib of Kensington. 'I wish it were under better circumstances. I have reason to believe that Camelot is in grave danger.'

The crowd began to mutter. Calib's ears perked up. Did Queen Guinevere know about the threat of another war with the Darklings?

'I have looked into Merlin's Mirror and seen signs that trouble me greatly—'

'Bah, that old Merlin was a charlatan and a crook,' Sir Kay interrupted. 'I never saw his so-called magic with my own eyes!'

Queen Guinevere ignored the interruption. 'We need to bring Arthur home as soon as possible. We have been vulnerable for too long.'

'With all due respect, Your Majesty,' said one adviser whose face sagged with wrinkles, 'there has been peace for years. We have no reason to suspect that there is any danger at all.'

Suddenly, the door to the throne room burst open as though a violent gust of wind had blown in.

'I beg an audience with the Round Table!'

The loud cry turned every head. Calib tilted forward on the ledge to get a better look.

A Two-Legger in worn leathers and a knit cap stood in the doorway. His face glistened with sweat, and his eyes roved around wildly as he gasped for breath. The man was in such disarray that it took Calib a moment before he recognised him as the local woodcutter, Gareth. He delivered firewood to all of Camelot, but he was not usually expected at the castle until noonday.

Two guards grabbed and held him back from reaching the queen, for he was still clutching his axe in his hand. 'A miracle! I must speak with the queen!' The man struggled to push past his captors.

'Release him,' Queen Guinevere said, raising her hand for order in the throne room. 'This man has kept us warm through many a winter. He may say whatever he wishes.'

'Thank you, Your Majesty. I bring news,' he gasped, still catching his breath. 'The Sword in the Stone has reappeared. I came upon it in a vale near the sea, just standing there as if it had grown out of the ground overnight!'

Calib froze, wondering if he was about to learn more about the legendary sword. Judging from the astounded gasps, the Two-Leggers were just as bewildered as he had been.

Queen Guinevere was the first to recover.

'There are signs of trouble everywhere, it seems,' she said grimly. 'The Sword in the Stone appears only in Britain's greatest hour of need.'

One of the knights jeered. 'Right. And whoever frees it next will be king!'

Angry murmurs rippled around the room.

'That's treason you're talking about!'

'Is it really? We haven't heard from King Arthur in months. Perhaps it is he who has abandoned us.'

Arguments began to break out.

The big-eared boy stepped half a pace nearer to Calib's spot on the ledge. This would be the perfect time to make his move, Calib thought, now that everyone was busy yelling.

Think like a Christopher. Think like a Christopher.

If the boy took one more step to the left, Calib might drop down neatly onto the boy's hat from above. But if he missed, it would be a very long fall to the flagstones below.

The boy took a shuffling step to the left to avoid being elbowed by a knight who was waving his arms around as he spoke.

Calib closed his eyes, curled into a ball, and rolled off the ledge . . .

Hurtling down, down for what seemed like forever . . .

Before landing lightly on the soft brim of the hat.

Calib's head spun as he righted himself. He could

not tell if he had just been laughably stupid or startlingly brave.

Calib scooted over to the owl feather. He grabbed it and pulled hard, but it would not come free. He examined the feather closely and saw that it was secured on to the boy's hat with thread. Calib carefully placed his teeth around the thread and began to nibble. As he chewed, the entire hat began to tip. Calib clung to the fabric. He realised with horror that the boy was reaching for his hat.

Calib pulled the thread with all his might, but the feather was still too tightly sewn. Calib ducked behind the feather and prayed the boy's hand wouldn't stray too close to him.

'Galahad, why have you stopped serving?' snapped Sir Edmund.

'Sorry, sir,' Galahad said politely. 'My hat is itchy.'

'I'd expect more fortitude from Lancelot's son,' grumbled the old knight. 'No wonder you ended up in the kitchen.'

This is Sir Lancelot's son? I'm sitting on Lancelot's son, Galahad? Calib was a little awestruck. No wonder the boy had arrived at the castle under Lancelot's banners. Regaining his wits, Calib ducked out from beneath the feather and continued to gnaw at the troublesome thread. He didn't see Galahad drop the date. He only felt a sudden vertigo as Galahad squatted down to retrieve it. He held onto the feather for dear life as it tilted forward dangerously.

Calib felt a shadow fall over him. He looked up. A craggy Two-Legger's nose almost brushed against Calib's whiskers.

All the colour drained out of Sir Edmund's face. He began choking on his date. Alarmed, Galahad stood again and thumped the knight across the back. Sir Edmund coughed. The date shot from his mouth, catapulted across the Round Table, and hit a sleepy-eyed adviser on the forehead.

The old knight took a few ragged breaths, and his face turned rumpled and red.

'Are you all right, sir?' Galahad asked.

'Raaaaaaaaaaaat!' Sir Edmund shouted, pointing a gnarled finger at Galahad.

Or rather, at Calib.

All eyes in the court zeroed in on him.

With a loud squeak, Calib leaped off Galahad's hat and onto the table, kicking the plate of dates on his way down. The platter flipped and clattered to the ground violently. Dried dates fell around

Calib like boulders. Sugar showered the table in a white cascade, covering him with it.

Calib dashed across the glittering surface, praying he wouldn't be struck by a stray date. The air was filled with thunderous explosions of shouting. Blood pounded in his ears. He had never been so scared in his life.

Wrinkled hands reached out to snatch him, but he dodged them one by one. He ran towards the queen and skidded to a stop at the table's edge. It was a long drop to the floor, and he was sure he wouldn't make it without breaking something.

'What in the . . . ?'

Calib sat up and looked at Queen Guinevere's surprised face. Panicked and confronted with Her Majesty, Calib did the only proper thing that came to mind: he stood on his hind legs and bowed deeply.

A nearby guard sprang forward, unsheathing his knife. He raised the blade high, ready to slam it down on Calib.

'Don't!' shouted Galahad. He leaped forward to block the guard's arm, but was only successful in pushing Sir Kay out of his seat.

There was a sudden flash of orange fur, and Calib found himself staring into the caramel eyes of a massive orange tabby cat. He caught a glimpse of white, needle-sharp teeth before the feline's jaws snapped shut around him.

Chapter Twenty-One

'Play dead,' the large cat whispered between her teeth.

Even though every instinct told him to fight, squeak, and run, Calib did as he was told and went limp.

'Lucinda, no!' cried the queen. 'Not on the Round Table!'

Queen Guinevere picked up her cat and placed her gently on the ground. Calib found himself unceremoniously carted through the throne room in Lucinda's mouth, which smelled distinctly of tuna. As Queen Guinevere's favourite pet, Lucinda was accustomed to fine seafood rather than mice.

Peeking through the gaps between Lucinda's sharp teeth, Calib could see Queen Guinevere dismissing the court. Calib bounced against the cat's rough tongue as she wound her way through an open door into the queen's private garden. She deposited him, shivering and saliva drenched, into a patch of dead rosebushes.

'Merlin bless you, Lucinda!' Calib gasped. He wiped long strings of spit from his face. Wet fur in a winter wind was a recipe for getting sick. 'You saved my life!'

Lucinda's squashed-in tabby-cat face gave her a permanent look of disgust. She bopped Calib on the head with a paw.

'Do you know how much trouble you mice have caused me today?' she hissed angrily. 'Stay out of trouble. Next time, I'm letting the knives fall where they may.'

'Yes, Lucinda,' Calib said as she bounded away. He knew her threat was an empty one. Lucinda was indebted to the Camelot mice. When she was a kitten, Lucinda had fallen into the queen's garden pond. Only the mice had responded to her mewlings for help. In gratitude, she had promised to always be their ally.

Calib waited until the cat was out of sight before he scoured the wall for a way to get back into the throne room. He had come so close to getting an owl feather!

He grabbed a nearby vine and began to scale the stone wall towards the stained-glass window with the missing pane. Huffing and puffing, Calib reached the ledge with throbbing paws. He peered in through the panel.

The throne room was now almost empty. Galahad was kneeling beneath the Round Table, picking up spilled dates that had rolled underneath. The quill was completely out in the open and ready for the snatching.

Calib squeezed through the empty pane and climbed onto the back of the throne, careful to avoid detection. Sliding down to the arm of the chair, Calib hopped onto the Round Table. A field of white sugar crystals lay before him like fresh snowfall. Calib darted and leaped into a nearby fruit bowl for cover.

One of Sir Kay's pages walked by, a surly-looking boy with thick brows. He made a point to scuff more sugar across the marble floor with his boots.

'Can't even hold a platter properly. Why did

anyone think you would ever hold a sword?' he sneered as he sauntered out of the room.

Galahad scowled but stayed silent as he went to fetch the mop. A tug of sympathy pulled at Calib's insides. It seemed to him that there were Warrens in just about every species. Plus, the Two-Legger had helped to free Valentina. And he'd tried to keep Calib from getting a knife to the tail.

Calib wanted to do something for this boy in return.

He had never talked to a human before, but he thought he would try now. Seeing his own paw prints in the sugar, an idea struck him. He took his tail and began to scratch out a short message in the sugar.

Once he was satisfied with what he had written, he turned his attention back to the quill. Yanking the feather from its stand on the Round Table and balancing it carefully across his shoulders, Calib hopped off the table and glided to the safety of the closest mouse tunnel.

As he floated to the ground, he remembered his grandfather's words to him in the tapestry hall:

You do not have to bear your burdens alone. 'Together in paw or tail, lest divided we fall and fail.'

In that moment, Calib decided he *would* ask Cecily to join him. An extra pair of eyes and paws on his quest could only help. His mission was too big and too important to do on his own – bigger, even, than becoming a squire.

Calib headed straight towards the training grounds, where the pages were sure to be practising, in preparation for whatever lay ahead. He felt a twinge of jealousy when he saw Devrin helping a first-year page with his grip on the wooden practice sword. He quickly turned away from them and scanned the arena for Cecily.

He saw Warren and Barnaby running laps – but no Cecily.

Her best friend, a kitchen maid named Ginny, however, was nearby. She was serving lunch – barley soup from a squash gourd.

'Greetings, Ginny!' Calib said brightly.

Ginny yelped and dropped her soup spoon, splattering both of them with broth.

'I don't know anything! So don't ask!' she squeaked, whiskers twitching.

'I only wanted to see if you've talked to Cecily today,' Calib said, confused by her behaviour.

All at once, Ginny burst into big, gasping tears. She swiped her tail across her eyes to mop them up.

'I'm sorry, Calib. I told her it was a bad idea, but she wouldn't listen. I didn't think she was serious about going. I tried to stop her, I really did,' she said shakily.

Calib's stomach knotted into pretzels.

'What are you talking about?' he asked. 'Where is she going?'

Ginny stared at him, more tears brimming in the corners of her brown eyes.

'She's gone to see the owls.'

Chapter Twenty-Two

Since the message had appeared mysteriously in the spilled sugar on the Round Table, Galahad had been puzzling over its author.

Great powar in small worriers.

Strange things had been happening – the fire in the scrying glass, the return of the sword, and now these words appearing from nowhere. He thought they must all be connected, but he couldn't figure out *how*. Like a song that wouldn't go out of his head, he repeated the message under his breath. Who could have placed it there?

A part of Galahad thought he might be going

crazy. The room had been empty when he began mopping. Galahad had made sure of that so he would not have to wipe up anyone's shoe prints again.

And his only theory sounded ridiculous even in his head. He did not dare say it out loud.

He was muddling through the task of preparing Sir Edmund's lunch of mashed prunes and honey when a clamour of excited voices came from the hallway. As the voices moved closer to the kitchen, Galahad paused in his work and looked up. Bors, one of the younger pages, ran into the kitchen.

'Aren't you coming? Everyone is going to try their luck pulling out the Sword in the Stone!' he said to Galahad.

'No, thanks,' Galahad said. 'I have no interest in seeing a bunch of old peacocks showing off.'

'Well, the good news is, even Sir Edmund is going too, so you don't have to make his lunch.' Bors scrunched his nose at the unappetising mush. 'Might as well come watch that cranky goat make a fool of himself!'

Grudgingly, Galahad allowed himself to be pulled along into the crowd funnelling out towards the mysterious Sword in the Stone. As they wound their way through town, more and more people joined the parade, until Galahad was squeezed on all sides by excited locals.

According to legend, the Sword in the Stone had last appeared before King Arthur was born, shortly after the Saxons had taken over Britain. It had sat there for many years, resisting anyone who tried to pull it out – young or old, strong or weak. Its inscription teased: 'Whoso pulleth out this sword of this stone and anvil is rightwise King born of all England.'

By the time young Arthur was working as a squire for his foster brother, Sir Kay, the sword had been all but forgotten – a passing oddity. It wasn't until Arthur yanked it out as a substitute sword for Sir Kay to use in his tournament that anyone remembered what it meant.

Life for Arthur had never been the same after that. He grew up to become the greatest king England had ever known, uniting all of Britain under one rule and defeating King Lot and the Saxons.

Most of Camelot had crowded around the meadow by the time Galahad and Bors arrived at this marvel. The crush of people prevented them from getting close enough to clearly see the sword. Galahad could identify only a few of the knights from their coats of arms.

'Do you see anything?' Bors asked, jumping in place to peek over everyone's heads. 'Who's next?'

Raising himself on his tiptoes and squinting, Galahad described for Bors each attempt at pulling the sword. Sir Kay tried to yank it until his face became beet red. Another knight threw his back out. Grumpy Sir Edmund took only a few tugs before he started making his squire do it on his behalf.

Galahad shook his head. When he was growing up, his mother had told him wondrous tales of knights and their incredible feats. Lady Elaine had sent him to Camelot so that he might follow in his father's footsteps. But to see these selfish old men seeking glory for themselves . . . It felt like a terrible betrayal. This was not how a knight should behave.

Remembering the fire in the scrying glass, Galahad knew Camelot needed a hero more than ever – but it certainly wasn't going to be any of these so-called knights.

Chapter Twenty-Three

Wearing the feather strapped across his back with twine, Calib dashed towards the drawbridge. He had to get out of the castle before anyone saw him. Using the ramparts to bypass any Two-Leggers, he felt his muscles burn, as if he'd run ten laps around the training grounds.

He had to get to Cecily, fast. She was in mortal danger.

Below him, a steady stream of Two-Leggers headed out of the castle, from lowly servants to all the knights. From the snatches of conversation that Calib overheard, it sounded like most of them were going to see the miraculous Sword in the Stone. Luckily for Calib, they would have to pass near St Getrude's ruins to do so.

Leaping onto the stable roof, he spied a squire ambling forward on a horse. He reined up just below Calib, where the boy waited for an oxcart to move out of the way. Sliding down carefully on the frosty thatching, Calib poised himself over the saddlebag full of oats. With a running leap, the mouse glided nimbly into it. Calib quickly buried himself and the feather deeper into the grain.

The ride through the village was uncomfortable. The oats scratched against his fur, and the jostling of the saddle made him feel sick to his stomach. But he didn't care. He was too focused on saving Cecily. He needed to stop her from reaching the owls' nests alone and without a feather.

And then, somehow, he would need to get Merlin's Crystal from the owls and convince them to take him to Leftie's lair before the mouse army marched. Calib knew what he had to do – but he had no idea *how* he would do it.

Just before Sir Kay and the rest of the travellers reached the beginning of the Darkling Woods, Calib clambered out of the sack and grabbed hold of a passing branch. He swung free of the cart and landed with a plop in a soft mound of snow, the ruins of St Gertrude rising from between the bare trees like towering tombstones.

Years before, the site had been a thriving monastery. Then one day, ships flying red flags with white dragons appeared on the horizon, bringing the first Saxon invaders. The Saxons landed ashore and took a torch to the cathedral and then to the rest of Britain. All that remained of the once-grand establishment were charred walls and blackened eaves.

Calib surveyed the ruins but found no evidence of owls. His heart sank. He knew from Macie that many owls had been migrating of late. Had they just been passing through? Suddenly, his footpaw sank into something with a sickening crunch. He looked down. He had placed a paw directly through the skull of an unidentifiable rodent.

Horrified, Calib fell backwards and shook his foot as hard as he could. The skull flew off and disappeared into a snowbank. Calib's heart thumped. He pushed away his nausea and the most horrible of thoughts.

He had to stop Camelot from marching upon the wrong enemy. If he couldn't track down the owls, he would have to get the owls to track him.

'Hello! Are there any owls here? Hoo! Hoo! I need to speak with you!' He hopped up and down, waving the feather above him, hoping to draw attention to himself.

A blur of white flashed in the corner of Calib's eye. A tree branch creaked. The mouse whipped around. Nothing.

He didn't see the giant shadow from above until it was already on top of him. A claw hooked on to the feather, and another yanked him aloft by a leg.

'Hey! Let go of me!' Calib shouted.

'It would be my pleasure. But your immediate death would displease the general,' said his captor. 'He likes to play with his prey first.'

Calib twisted around and looked up into two yellow eyes, each as big as the mouse's head. A snowy owl glared down at him. Its white-and-black feathers blended perfectly with the stark surroundings. Calib's plan had worked far better than he had hoped.

Too well, judging by the pinched feel of the owl's talons around Calib's leg.

Calib quickly looked away, only to realise he had been carried many feet above the ground in a matter of seconds.

He gulped and squeezed his eyes shut. 'Look! I have an owl feather! You *have* to listen to what I have to say.' He struggled to shout against the rushing wind.

'We'll let General Gaius decide what to do with you,' the owl replied coldly.

The owl suddenly loosened his grip and let Calib fall.

Before Calib had a chance to scream, he tumbled into a nest sitting high on a ruined wall. The pile of twigs had been hidden between two snow embankments that kept it invisible from the ground.

Calib was grateful that his landing was somewhat cushioned by a soft burlap sack.

'Oww! My tail!'

Calib jumped back, surprised to hear the burlap sack speak to him.

'Cecily?' he asked, recognising the muffled voice.

'Calib, is that you?' the sack responded.

Calib quickly untied the knot cinching the bag together, revealing Cecily's head. Her fur was matted and dirty, but she seemed otherwise uninjured.

'You're alive!' exclaimed Calib. Relief wrapped around him like a blanket.

'Of *course* I'm alive,' Cecily said irritably. She

struggled out of the bag. 'Be careful,' she whispered sharply. 'They'll hear you.'

'Who?' Calib asked.

'Hoo?' came the soft reply from behind.

Calib slowly turned around.

Three baby owls were watching Calib and Cecily with saucer-round eyes. Even though they had yet to shed the down feathers of their nest days, they still gripped the edge of the nest with wickedly curved claws. The middle owlet hopped forward.

'Hoo?' It gave Calib a quick peck on the head.

'Stop that!' Calib shooed the owlet away with a swoop of the feather. 'I am a diplomat!'

'Are you now?' a new voice drawled. An imperious great horned owl landed at the edge of the nest. The wind from his wings nearly knocked Calib over.

Its yellow eyes, surrounded by black feathers, glowed like miniature suns above a sharp, curved beak. Calib could hardly look at it without trembling, imagining how easily the beak would pierce his flesh. Seeing the red sash across the owl's chest, Calib knew immediately who this owl must be: General Gaius Thornfeather.

The owl snapped his beak sharply, and the owlets hastily retreated.

'But General Gaius,' one of them whined. 'I never get to play with the food!'

'Away, cadets.' General Gaius snapped his beak again. The severe look on the horned owl meant business, and the three owlets quickly took wing and glided in the direction of another turret.

Then the general turned his attention to Calib and Cecily, twisting his head around so quickly that the mice jumped back.

'I have led my parliament for more years than the feathers on my wings, and I have seen a lot of things,' Gaius began, his ear tufts arching tyrannically. 'But never have I seen such stupid behaviour from fur-beasts!'

His vivid eyes took them in from paws to ears. Calib hoped Cecily couldn't hear his teeth chattering.

'Sneaking about our nests and raising a racket for all the woodlands to hear!'

He swivelled to glare at Calib. 'I shall slay you where you stand!'

The owl let out an earsplitting screech. He spread his wings in an attack pose and then swept them down forcefully, toppling Calib and Cecily onto the nest floor. Calib rolled to the side as Gaius snapped at his tail. He had only a split second to act before the owl would attack again.

Without thinking, the mouse brought the nib of the quill crashing down on the owl's beak as General Gaius went for another vicious peck.

'Not so fast!' Calib shouted at the top of his lungs, holding up the feather shaft like a sword. It shook in his paws. General Gaius reared back from the blow, stunned. As for Calib, he felt as surprised as the general looked.

'Please,' Calib pleaded. He put down the quill and offered it to the owl, bowing his head. 'My grandfather, Commander Yvers Christopher, has been murdered. Terrible things are at work in Camelot. We need your help.'

There was a long silence. Calib was almost too afraid to look up; too afraid that the sight of the vicious owl swooping down on him would be his last.

'Yvers is murdered?' the owl asked at last.

Calib nodded. After another pause, General Gaius lowered his wings.

'I always said the Christophers were a flighty, foolhardy bunch,' General Gaius said. 'But let no beast say the owls do not honour the Feather Offering. Follow me.'

Chapter Twenty-Four

Strong gusts of wind whipped up around them. Calib and Cecily clutched each other's tails to avoid getting blown away. They balanced precariously on top of the slippery stone walls while Gaius rapped his beak on the window of St Gertrude's tallest turret.

'Thaddeus,' the owl said. 'We have visitors from Camelot who seek your counsel.'

There was silence at first, but then a voice, as creaky as a worn-out rocking chair, came from inside: 'Enter.'

A wizened old barn owl nested in the shadows

of the small tower. His white, heart-shaped face turned towards them. Milky cataracts filled the owl's shiny black eyes like constellations.

Calib held back a gasp, for the owl wore a strange-looking necklace, a dagger-shaped crystal on a chain. It glittered against his feathers like a fallen star. Carved from the clearest diamond, it was about the length of Calib's arm – Merlin's Crystal.

Awe buoyed Calib's hopes. Here was one of the last magical treasures left in the land. Perhaps it could save them yet.

'I am Thaddeus of the Fellwater Swamps.' The barn owl introduced himself, bowing with his wings outspread. From wingtip to wingtip, they stretched the length of the room.

'Cecily von Mandrake,' Cecily said, dipping into a curtsy.

'A-and I'm Calib Christopher,' Calib croaked, his eyes still entranced by the crystal.

'Well met, groundlings.'

General Gaius strutted forward. 'The fur-beasts say that Commander Yvers has been murdered by an assassin,' he said.

Thaddeus bowed his large head. 'So it is as I feared, then. A great evil has come upon Camelot.'

'Then you know who is responsible for my grandfather's murder?' Calib's pulse quickened beneath his fur.

'Not by name,' the barn owl replied, and Calib felt a heavy wave of disappointment. 'My Sight grows dimmer year by year.'

'You're a Seer?' Cecily asked in wonder. Seers were animals who, though physically blind, could predict the future.

'Old Magic isn't what it once was, and our foe is powerful,' Thaddeus said. 'The future is clouded, but I know one thing: though this is a new threat, this is not a new enemy.'

Calib felt the fur along his neck rise up strand by strand, and the tip of his tail twitched.

'There is more,' Thaddeus added with a creak in his voice. 'I've forseen the downfall of Camelot.'

'But there must be some way to stop it!' Cecily cried.

'The Sight is never wrong, fur-beast,' General Gaius said, and Calib thought he heard a new emotion in the owl's voice: pity. 'What Thaddeus Sees always comes to be.'

'You are forgetting, General,' Thaddeus said. His sightless eyes turned towards Calib. 'Once, the action of a single mouse changed the tide of a vision.'

A shiver raced up Calib's spine. Could Thaddeus be talking about his father?

'Camelot believes that the Darklings are behind Commander Yvers's death,' Calib said, hoping his voice was steady. 'And we have declared war on them. But if the Darklings did not kill my grandfather, then we are fighting the wrong enemy.'

Calib took a deep breath. His next words came out in a rush.

'Please, if you could lend us Merlin's Crystal and take us to Leftie's lair in the Slate Rocks, we might be able to reason with the Darklings before Camelot gets there, and then together turn our attention on our *true* enemy!'

'The Darklings!' General Gaius hunched his wings and let out an angry screech. 'I will eat my own feathers before I help that sorry lot! The Darklings are the reason why we fled the Fellwater Swamps in the first place.'

'What do you mean?' Calib asked, his stomach sinking.

'Leftie grew desperate and attacked us,' Thaddeus said. 'He believed that the crystal would help him defend the woods from whatever has been stealing their food.'

'And why should we lend Merlin's Crystal to

them when they couldn't keep their own treasure safe?' Gaius interjected, referring to the mirror that the Darklings had lost years ago.

'But the Darklings are *starving*,' Cecily interjected. 'We met a Darkling crow, and she was as skinny as a reed. How can you do nothing while other creatures suffer?'

Thaddeus shook his head sadly. 'You don't understand. When Merlin left us owls in charge of his crystal, he gave us a riddle to accompany it. Only the creature who correctly answers it may use the crystal. Leftie has tried to solve the riddle many times and has always failed. The last time that happened, he tried to take the crystal by force instead.'

'Then let us try the riddle,' Cecily asked, crossing her arms. Calib swallowed hard and hoped Cecily knew what she was doing.

Thaddeus considered this for a moment before nodding once.

'Very well,' he said, and cleared his throat. 'The riddle: "I grow strong when the strong grow weak. I blind more than the darkest night or the brightest sun. When the brave lack me, they are fools. When fools gain me, they are wise. What am I?"'

Cecily began pacing the turret, mumbling to herself as Calib twisted his paws.

'Does this have anything to do with training exercises?' Cecily asked.

'Waste of our time,' General Gaius scoffed. 'Let us feed them to the owlets already.'

'Patience, Gaius.' Thaddeus's blind eyes seemed to stare at Calib.

Calib closed his eyes so that he could focus better. Grandfather Yvers had loved puzzles and riddles, but Calib didn't seem to have inherited his grandfather's gift for them. From the stories he shared with Calib in the tapestry hall before the tournament, it seemed Calib had only inherited Yvers's knack for trouble.

'Wait a whisker . . .' Calib piped up. Commander Yvers had told Calib something else that morning, too. *Being brave is not about lacking fear.*

'The answer is fear!' Calib burst out. General Gaius blinked quickly while Cecily frowned.

'Listen,' Calib said hurriedly. 'Fear grows strong when the strong grow weak. It blinds more than sunlight or darkness. When the brave lack fear, they are fools! When fools learn to fear, they are wise!'

General Gaius and Thaddeus looked at each other. Cecily let out a big whoop.

'He's right! Calib's right! It fits!'

'You are correct,' Thaddeus said, a smile playing at the corner of his beak. 'Merlin's Crystal is yours to use as you see fit, Calib Christopher.'

Gaius's eyes looked like they might pop out of his gigantic head. 'You're going to give one of Merlin's greatest treasures to two fur-beasts barely out of their nursing days? They can barely lift it between the two of them!'

'And that's why you shall accompany them, Gaius Thornfeather.' Thaddeus turned to face Gaius. 'You will carry the crystal for them while it serves Calib's purpose, and fly them to Leftie's lair.'

General Gaius's ear tufts rose in irritation.

'And what if I refuse?' General Gaius asked, narrowing his eyes. 'What happens to Camelot or the Darklings is none of our concern. We look after our own.'

'You helped my father in Camelot's greatest hour of need once, at the Battle at Rickonback River,' Calib said. He felt young again, like a small mousling asking for just one more piece of rhubarb pie or one more tale about Sir Samuel Snaggletooth before bed. 'I only ask that you heed that call again, in Sir Trenton's name!'

'So, now you want to warn your father's enemy

of Camelot's attack?' Gaius asked sceptically. He had puffed his feathers so that he was now twice his usual size.

'I want to do what's right,' Calib answered. 'It's what my father would have wanted. The Darklings are innocent!'

'Whatever is out there stealing from the Darklings probably killed Commander Yvers,' Cecily added. 'If it is not stopped now, what's to stop it from coming after you?'

'They are right,' Thaddeus said. 'The mousling has answered the riddle correctly. We must abide by Merlin's wishes. This is the course of fate, Gaius. You would be foolish to fly against such winds.'

Gaius rapped his talons on the ground as he considered everyone's points. Though Calib wanted to look away, he forced himself to stare into the owl's domineering eyes. He didn't know what he would do if Gaius didn't agree.

'I will take you to Leftie's lair in the foothills of the Iron Mountains, and I will carry the crystal for you,' the owl said finally. 'But take heed, Calib Christopher. You will owe the owls a favour. A *big* one. And when the time comes for us to collect, you may wish you had not agreed.'

Chapter Twenty-Five

Settled securely in a small basket dangling from General Gaius's talons, Calib and Cecily watched the nest shrink away into a small brown dot on top of a snow-covered stone wall. Before them, the wider forest opened like an immense, sugar-frosted dessert.

Calib's fear melted away to wonder. He had known the world was vast from studying the library's many maps, but seeing it all spread out beneath him was something else entirely. As Gaius lifted them higher and higher above the trees, Calib could make out the mountains in the faraway distance. The formations rose up over the horizon like a tidal wave of stone. Somewhere far, far below them were the Slate Rocks, Leftie's home. Beside Calib, Cecily clutched the side of the basket tightly and squeezed her eyes shut.

'The Iron Mountains,' Calib whispered. The grey-coloured mountain range marked the farthest edge of their land. No mouse had ever crossed those ridges and come back to tell the tale.

'Aye,' the general said in his clipped voice. 'The known woodland realm ends there.'

Taking a deep breath, Calib called up to the bird. 'Did you ever know my father personally?' he asked quickly, before his courage left him.

'I was a lieutenant the day Sir Trenton met with General Thaddeus,' he said as his large wings caught an extra gust of wind.

'What was he like?' Calib pressed.

'He was as stupid as you were this afternoon,' General Gaius said over the noise of the wind. 'But Merlin won us over to his cause. In the end, your father sacrificed much to protect those he cared for most. And for that, we remember him as a hero.'

Pride swelled in Calib's heart. 'Thank you,' he whispered.

As the owl continued his flight towards the mountains, Calib marvelled at Merlin's Crystal. It dangled from Gaius's neck, just out of reach. The light from the setting sun made the crystal glow a fiery red. It almost looked like an ember against Gaius's feathered breast.

Lulled by the crystal's dancing light, Calib found himself nodding off. He hadn't had much sleep the previous night, and the wicker basket rocked gently in the wind.

In his half-dreams, he stood before his parents' tapestry. Sir Trenton was holding out Merlin's Crystal to him. If only he could reach out and take it. Calib grasped the one end of the crystal but could not pull it free. It was stuck half in the tapestry, half out. The earth began to tremble from underneath him, just like it had the day that Galahad arrived.

Calib woke and realised it was Cecily shaking him gently awake.

'We're almost there,' she said.

'How long was I asleep?' Calib asked, rubbing his eyes.

'Not long,' Cecily said, but Calib could tell she was lying. She hesitated. 'You were mumbling in your sleep.'

He scrubbed a paw in his eyes, trying to get the sleep out.

The general swooped below the treeline, expertly avoiding the branches as he brought them to the banks of a river. He gently lowered the basket to the ground. Cecily wobbled out unsteadily, looking relieved.

'Are we getting close to Leftie's lair?' Calib squinted into the twilight as he too hopped out of the basket.

'We're at the farthest edge of the Darkling Woods,' General Gaius said. 'But now it's getting dark, and even the owls don't dare approach the Darkling lair before daybreak. We will make camp and wait until morning.'

'But what about the Camelot army?' Cecily asked. 'The mice left Camelot hours ago!'

Gaius chuckled. 'The slowest owl flies twice as fast as the speediest Camelot mouse. It will take your army a full-day's march to get to Leftie.' Gaius swivelled his head around to survey the area. 'We make camp here, and quietly. We're in Berwin Featherbane's territory now.'

'Berwin the Beastly is still alive?' Calib asked, taken aback. All the mice of Camelot had heard the stories. Berwin was once one of King Lot's fighting bears, trained by Two-Leggers to battle other animals for entertainment. He'd earned many scars on his body but never lost a fight. When King Arthur defeated Lot and heard about Berwin, he commanded that the bear be freed.

But Berwin did not forgive easily.

The bear began to terrorise the surrounding lands – stealing sheep and killing every creature at will. He was finally driven across Rickonback River to live his days in isolation. He was the kind of villain the nursemaids used to scare mouslings into following the rules. *Go to sleep, little mousling, or Berwin the Beastly will gobble you whole.*

'Berwin's den is just down this river,' General Gaius said. 'Leftie chose to make the Slate Rocks the Darkling headquarters *precisely* because they're close to Berwin. Even though the bear is a danger to the Darklings, he's also a danger to everyone else, so he keeps intruders at bay. Military genius,' the owl said. Calib thought he could detect a hint of admiration for the lynx's tactics. 'Be on your guard.'

The owl ducked his head, and with his beak unclipped a small mouse-sized rapier from his sash. He offered it to Cecily. 'Here's your weapon back.'

'Thank you,' she said, retrieving it from his beak

with a nervous smile. 'I'm sorry I nearly took out your eye earlier.'

'You'll need those lightning reflexes if you want to survive these woods,' Gaius said. 'Now, promise to stay hidden until I come back for you.'

Calib gulped. 'You're *leaving*?'

'I've flown for hours, and I'm hungry,' the general said. 'I must go and hunt for my dinner, and I may count on many more long hours before I find anything to eat. Food has been . . . hiding . . . the last few days.'

A queasy feeling blossomed in Calib's gut. 'You mean . . . hunt for nuts and berries?'

General Gaius snapped his beak in amusement. 'Something like that,' the owl said. 'I'll be back before dawn.'

'And what about Merlin's Crystal?' Cecily said. 'How do we know you're not just abandoning us to Berwin?'

'Guess you'll just have to trust me.' Gaius smirked and then took off silently into the darkening sky. It was a deep dusk, a kind of twilight that made the trees blend into a continuous tangle of snowy brambles.

'Wait! Come back!' Calib shouted, watching Gaius fly out of sight. His breath came out in small white puffs. The dangers of their predicament swiftly became apparent. They had just been abandoned in unfamiliar woods on a cold winter's night, and there was no crystal to distract Leftie with if the Darkling scouts *did* show up.

'It's not like we have any choice but to trust him,' Cecily said, letting out a long sigh. 'Did you bring any camping gear? Blankets? Any food?'

'No,' he admitted, feeling wholly underprepared. His stomach growled noisily, as if in response. It had been hours since the council meeting that morning. He thought about how angry Madame von Mandrake would be when she discovered that they were missing from supper. Only Macie's scouts were ever excused from dinner for patrol duties.

'Macie!' Calib exclaimed suddenly, causing Cecily to jump. 'Why didn't I think of that before? Macie's scouts bury their food supplies throughout these woods! They mark the hiding places with a special sign, like this.' He scratched a small arrow symbol in the frozen dirt.

Cecily puffed out her cheeks. 'Well, that's something, at least. Come on!'

They set off along the riverbank, looking for shelter and listening to the endless murmur of water. Occasionally, thin sheets of ice floated by on the river. Calib wondered if Valentina had made it back to her clan yet.

'Thank you for coming after me,' Cecily said. Her paws crunched in the frost. 'I know I should have waited, but I was afraid of missing out on the action.'

'It's all right. I'm just glad I made it in time,' Calib said. A warmth spread through him that was at odds with the chill in the air. 'You were brave to go out on your own.'

She flashed him a quick smile, and they lapsed into a comfortable silence.

He and Cecily wandered farther away from the river, examining each tree. Finally, just before the last of the sun was extinguished, they spotted a stand of birch trees, one of them scored with Macie's special sign.

They began digging furiously, arcs of dirt flying out behind them. Cecily jumped back and pulled out a dirty knapsack from the hole she had dug. 'Wow, Macie buries these things deep!'

'Please say she packed dried cherries,' Calib said with a hungry groan.

Cecily's eyes were wide when she peered up at him. 'It's empty.'

Calib's fur raised, and a smell came to his nose

– something foreign. Something large. 'Someone else has been here,' he whispered.

'Well,' Cecily said, dumping the empty bag back into the hole. 'I hope you have another brilliant plan baking in your brain, because I'm fresh out.'

'Working on it,' Calib said, chewing on his whiskers. As he circled to the other side of the tree, the musky odour grew stronger.

'Cecily, come over here and take a whiff of this,' he said.

'Blech, Calib, that's not funny,' Cecily said as she came around the tree. Her snout wrinkled in disgust. 'If you're just going to break wind all night—'

'It wasn't me,' Calib protested. 'Try again.'

Cecily took another sniff, this time concentrating harder on the garlicky odour. 'It smells like, like . . .'

'Weasel musk,' they whispered together.

In their early days of training, Sir Owen had taught them all to recognise the scents of various animals, especially the ones who had a taste for mice. Once they became squires, he said, they would have to rely on their noses to determine who was friend or foe.

Weasels were definitely the latter.

Chapter Twenty-Six

'I don't understand,' Cecily said. Calib could hear his own panic in her voice. 'Weasels haven't been in Britain in years and years.'

'I know,' Calib whispered. 'But it's *definitely* weasel musk.' His ears prickled. Even his tail felt stiff with anxiety. 'The weasels must be close.'

'We should see what they're up to,' Cecily said.

They ducked under an elderberry bush, with ice clinging to its branches, and fought their way through a tangle of brambles. Calib's nose was twitching, and his eyes watered from the stench.

The musk grew much stronger. Calib stopped

short. Peering around, he saw a small fire burning through the trees. There was not a creature in sight. Calib motioned to Cecily, and she nodded. Together, they quietly approached the clearing from behind a small foothill.

Cecily jabbed Calib in the ribs.

'Look!' she said under her breath.

What they had thought was a small hill was actually a towering stockpile of foodstuffs. Everything from satchels of dried berries and acorns to slabs of dried honeycomb and fish were heaped in a large mound.

'There must be enough food here to last an entire winter,' Cecily whispered, her eyes round with awe.

'What do you want to bet that it's all been stolen?' Calib thought of Valentina and her hungry tribe.

'Do you hear that?' Cecily's soft ears quivered, trying to catch what she was hearing. There was nothing but stillness and then . . .

Calib gasped. 'Are those . . . *Two-Legger* voices?' he asked, shock making his voice louder than he intended. 'What are the Two-Legger knights doing so deep in the Darkling forest?'

Cecily shook her head. 'I don't think they are from Camelot.'

Cautiously, Calib crept towards the stockpile and peered around it. A strange shimmering in the air seemed to separate them from an army of a hundred men and women gathered around in groups, their weapons gleaming in the light of several campfires. Calib found it hard to look at the group directly.

In the flickering glow, Calib could just make out the flags on top of the armies' tents: white dragons against a red backing.

The Saxons were back in Britain.

Calib was stunned. At last, everything made sense: the owls' migration, the crows' fear, the forest stripped of food.

At last, he could give a name to the evil advancing towards Camelot.

Suddenly, something grabbed Calib from behind and pinned his arms behind him. He saw another shape lunge out from the shadows for Cecily.

'Cecily, watch out!'

A smelly bag was thrown over his head. He could hear wicked laughter around him.

'Well, look at what we have here – a coupl'a mousling thieves!' one of his captors cackled in a strange accent. 'Dumb ones, too, walking down-wind like that – could smell them from a mile away! They'll fetch a grand ransom, indeed!'

The weasel scent was as strong as it had ever been, and Calib knew without a doubt that it was weasels who had found them.

'Take them to the Manderlean first!' hissed another voice.

'Aye, he will know what to do with them,' the first voice replied. Then it let out a sharp yelp.

'Aiiiii! This one's got a sword!' it shouted. 'Help!'

A tussle began to unfold just a few feet from Calib. He could hear more shouts of pain as Cecily made quick use of her weapon. His training taking over, Calib head-butted his captor hard in the chin and shoved him off-balance.

Ripping the bag from his head, he saw Cecily taking on a weasel with a torn ear. Blood already trickled from a gash on the weasel's side. He held a cutlass and was swiping at Cecily, who deflected each attack. Calib's captor – also a weasel, but with a tufted tail – was still bent over, winded.

Calib charged Tuft-Tail, sack in paw. He pulled the bag over the weasel's head and pushed the creature to the ground. The weasel dropped the cutlass. Calib ran back towards Cecily.

But Cecily was already headed in his direction.

'Run!' she shouted to Calib. 'To the river!'

He reached out and grabbed Cecily's outstretched

paw. Together, they sprinted as fast as they could through the trees. Calib couldn't see anything. Any second, he expected to run into a wayward branch or trip over a rock.

Behind them, the voices of their pursuers grew louder.

'They're gaining!' Calib gasped. His legs would not be able to keep up very much longer with Cecily's sprinting. His pace began to slow.

'Calib, come on!' Cecily pulled at his arm, urging him to keep up.

Calib heard a crackling from underneath them. They were walking on nothing but thin twigs criss-crossed over a giant hole.

'Cecily, wait!'

It was too late. The ground gave way underneath their paws. With a loud snap, they plunged into darkness.

Cecily and Calib landed on the spongy forest floor a few feet below. Disoriented, Calib saw they had fallen into a trap.

'What is this?' Cecily whispered. Calib shushed her and pulled them both against the closest wall.

What little moonlight shining in from above was snuffed out. An enormous shadow loomed above and then scooped them up with a massive paw.

Chapter Twenty-Seven

Calib and Cecily were frozen, momentarily speechless as they stared snout-to-snout with their fearsome and gigantic captor.

Berwin Featherbane. Berwin the Beastly, the Vicious, the Cruel.

The bear appeared unimpressed with his catch. His glittering eyes narrowed with confusion. He sniffed at the two mice in his paw.

'Say something,' whispered Cecily through her teeth.

'H-Hello, Master Berwin,' Calib stuttered.

The bear growled, a deep rumbling that seemed

to vibrate through his entire body. He puffed a gust of hot, fishy breath into their faces and tossed Calib and Cecily into the burlap sack he had been carrying over his shoulder. They tumbled around in the dark and landed alongside two dead trout.

'Well, that could have gone better,' Calib said, recoiling from the feel of the slick scales.

'We're going to reek for weeks – the smell will never come out of my fur!' lamented Cecily as she tried to balance on top of a fish eye. She slipped and landed with a plop.

If we get out of here, Calib nearly said. But he bit his tongue.

After much bouncing and jostling, Berwin came to a stop. The top of the bag opened, and all its contents pitched forward. Cecily and Calib spilled out, coughing and gasping for fresh air, into a wooden basin.

Calib peered through a crack in the wood. They had arrived in a cosy, underground den, circular in shape and insulated with wattle. The room was sparse and undecorated, except for a suit of bear-shaped armour that hung like a prized antique against the far wall.

Without a word, Berwin leaned down to rekindle a dying fire in the hearth. He took a pipe from the mantel and lit it using a piece of tinder. A new smell filled Calib's nose – sweet, dried dandelion smoke, the kind that his grandfather had liked to smoke after a stressful day of council meetings.

He could see Berwin clumsily puffing on the wooden pipe. The bear sat hunched on a stump, his paunch sagging over his thighs. His brown shaggy fur was matted, tangled, and tinged with grey hairs. Scores of pale scars raked across his back. Calib's heart ached at the sight of so many old wounds.

This was not the monster from the stories he had heard in his childhood. This was a forlorn and weary bear, sitting all alone in his cave.

Calib gathered his courage. 'Excuse me,' Calib squeaked from the basin. 'Can we ask you a question?'

'I only answer questions after I've had dinner,' the bear groused, not bothering to look at him. 'And you two make a pretty measly appetiser.'

Cecily gripped her rapier tightly, but Calib shook his head. They would never be able to use force against him. Calib climbed as high as he could onto the lip of the sink and cleared his throat.

'That's a shame,' Calib called out with forced casualness, 'because there's trouble coming to the woods, and you're going to need our help!'

'Ha!' Berwin replied. 'Your help. That's rich.' He shook his head. 'Besides, you don't know the half of it.'

'We know the Saxons are back,' Cecily said, climbing up next to Calib.

Berwin's ears perked up a bit. 'You've seen them too, eh?' He sniffed in their direction. 'I thought their little bit of cloaking magic had everyone fooled. You must have been able to slip right under it, as small as you are.'

'Magic?' Calib repeated. This, of all things, was not what he'd expected Berwin to say. There used be spells, but he had thought all magic had left Camelot when the Two-Legger wizard Merlin had gone missing.

Berwin nodded glumly.

'But the Saxons were driven off the island years ago,' Cecily said. 'Why are they back?'

'Same reason as before.' Berwin exhaled a cloud of smoke, so he looked like a smouldering dragon. 'Not enough food in their homeland. But unlike last time, now they advance on Camelot with vengeance in their hearts. They still blame Arthur for the death of King Lot. The Two-Leggers still believe that Britain belongs to them.'

A smoke ring floated above Calib's head,

bringing with it the memory of the enemy's camp-fires.

'They've also brought their weasels with them, to eat all the berries and kill all the fish,' Berwin continued. 'Weakening the Camelot Two-Leggers before they attack . . . and leaving me *extremely* hungry.'

'If all this is true,' Calib said slowly, 'we will need to work together to defeat the weasels first. We need the owls and the Darklings to stand together with Camelot! We need *you* as well!'

The bear made a sound halfway between a cough and a wheeze, and for a moment, Calib thought Berwin was choking. It was only when his upper lip curled back in a terrifying grin that Calib realised Berwin was laughing.

'If you two think there's any hope of change here in these old woods, then you're more foolish than I thought,' the bear said, swiping his eyes with a paw. 'The grudge between Camelot and the Darklings runs deeper than the roots of the oldest trees. That will never change.'

'We can't just sit here and do nothing,' Calib said hotly. 'Everyone's lives are at stake – Camelot and Darkling, man and animal, even yours!'

'My life has always been at stake.' The bear

waved his paw dismissively. 'Tell me something new.'

'I thought the bear was the symbol of bravery and strength,' Calib said, letting his temper get the better of him. 'It's a symbol painted on the Two-Legger shields. But you're . . . you're not brave at all!'

At this, Berwin stood and stormed towards the wooden basin. The ground shook underneath his gigantic paws. Seeing his fearsome yellow teeth bared, Calib and Cecily fell back against the fish, terrified.

'Don't speak of what you don't know!' Berwin roared, flecks of spittle hitting the mice like raindrops. His eyes were wild and full of pain. 'Bravery did me no good when the Two-Leggers killed my family! Caring did no good in the arena when I had to kill to survive!'

Calib had struck a raw nerve. The bear was seething, and his muzzle twisted with uncontrollable anger. Pity and fear swirled in Calib's gut.

'Why would I come to the defence of *men*?' Berwin continued to rage, spitting out his last word like a curse. 'They slaughter my kind for sport. With their ceaseless hunting . . . For all I know, I may be the last bear left!'

Berwin yelled so loudly, Calib and Cecily had to

cover their ears. He threw his pipe against the wall, and it cracked into two. Then he staggered towards the wall, leaning heavily against it, exhausted.

Calib's heart was humming in his throat. And despite their great difference in size, he thought he understood the bear, at least a little. As the last Christopher, he too could imagine what it felt like to lose so much. Berwin was not born a villain; he was *made* one.

'It's the right thing to do,' Calib said in a hushed voice. 'Because justice looks different from revenge.'

'King Arthur freed you . . . and he's a man,' Cecily chimed in.

'He should have killed me instead,' Berwin said hoarsely. He looked up at the mice, his eyes gleaming with some unspoken sadness. He picked up his broken pipe and threw it into the fireplace. 'Why bother with anything when you're the last of your kind?'

'There is always hope. If you help us, we'll help you find other bears.'

Berwin Featherbane looked at the two mice and heaved a big sigh. He stared at his old armour, his gaze lost in the trenches of some painful memory.

'Fight with us,' Calib pressed. 'Our futures depend on it.'

For a second, Berwin seemed to be considering it. Then he snarled.

'My future is simply my next meal,' Berwin said, licking his chops. 'And two bony mice are better than no mice.'

Calib became aware of the smoke and fish smell still lingering in his fur as Berwin's large black nose hovered above them. The bear inhaled deeply, and Calib hoped with all the pads on his paws that he and Cecily didn't smell like a well-cooked meal.

Suddenly, Berwin grabbed Calib and Cecily in one enormous claw, and Calib banged his nose against Cecily's head as the bear lumbered to the exit.

'What are you doing?' Cecily shouted, kicking her feet frantically. Calib grabbed pawfuls of the bear's wiry hair and yanked, but a mouse's strength was no match against a full-grown bear.

Then, without warning, the bear stopped. He dropped Calib and Cecily on the ground. Gasping, Calib rolled over onto his back and saw stars winking at him through the web of trees. They were out of Berwin the Beastly's den.

'It's been a long time since I've seen beasts with courage,' the bear said, his voice rough. 'I will not fight for Camelot – but I will not eat you, either. Not today, anyway.'

The old bear turned and shuffled back down the dark passage to his lonely home.

Hardly daring to believe it, Calib took a moment before he could find his voice.

'We'll come back!' he called after the lumbering shadow, his paws cupped around his mouth. 'We promised to help find more bears like you, and we will!'

But either Berwin didn't hear him, or he pretended not to, for the bear did not re-emerge.

Calib felt a tug on his cloak and looked over at Cecily to see the moon reflected in her wide, brown eyes.

'Calib,' she said, paw on her rapier's hilt. 'Where *are* we?'

Chapter Twenty-Eight

By the time Galahad reached the final steps to the aviary, he was out of breath. Located high in the chapel's bell tower, right below the bells themselves, the aviary housed a flock of larks that served as Camelot's fastest messengers.

As Galahad entered the turret, he marvelled at the hanging birdcages suspended by wires from the ceiling beams. He stood for a moment, mesmerised by the rustling of wings and soft coos of sleeping larks. It wasn't yet sunrise, and Galahad knew they wouldn't wake for a little while longer. Still, it was better to wait here for dawn than to toss and turn in his bed, haunted by dreams of fire and blood.

Stepping carefully around the bird droppings that littered the ground, Galahad unrolled a piece of parchment from his pocket. Holding it up to a flickering lantern, he double-checked his message to Sister Agatha for accuracy.

Sister Agatha was St Anne's head librarian and a precise grammarian. She would not take kindly to a message that was less than perfect, especially from her worst pupil. More than once, Galahad had been subjected to one of her fiery lectures on properly using commas. Nevertheless, Sister Agatha's library was pristinely kept and contained the most thorough account of the kingdom's history. If anyone could tell Galahad more about the Saxons, it would be her.

Galahad had tried the castle's library first, but Camelot did not have Sister Agatha to keep its records neat and organised. It seemed like mice had chewed through many of the pages related to the Saxons from the books and scrolls, making them unreadable.

After puzzling over whether to add a comma after 'sincerely', Galahad found himself staring out the window instead. The snow-covered hills of the countryside gave way to the barren forest. Beyond that, the sliver of the Iron Mountains crouched on the horizon like a hibernating bear.

Galahad sighed, his breath clouding in front of him. He wondered what it would have been like to run away. He wished he did not care about what happened to the castle and its people, but he knew what it felt like to be abandoned. In that way, he didn't want to be like his father.

Movement against the sky caught his eyes. Squinting, Galahad thought he could make out wings, but they were too small to belong to an owl. With a gasp, he realised it was a returning messenger lark struggling against the winter wind, which seemed determined to knock the bird out of the sky. It was highly unusual for a lark to fly in the night.

Galahad waved his arm out the window.

'Come on! You're almost here!'

The bird persevered. It alighted on the window ledge and promptly collapsed from exhaustion. Its chest heaving, the lark tried to kick off a tattered roll of parchment that was attached to its leg. Gently, Galahad removed the message. The paper was badly damaged by rain, and it was burned on one side.

Galahad carefully scooped up the tired bird and placed it in a cage filled with water and paper bedding before turning his attention back to the message.

Most of the ink had run together, but Galahad could make out three blurry words that turned him cold with dread: 'danger', 'rumours' and 'prepare'.

Chapter Twenty-Nine

They were lost – completely and hopelessly lost.

The only thing Calib was certain of was that they were now most definitely in Darkling territory.

'Let's try to find the river,' he said, picking a fish scale off his fur. 'When General Gaius doesn't find us, he'll probably look around the river-banks.'

'But which way?' Cecily asked, tucking her shivering paws into the folds of her cloak. 'If we choose incorrectly, we might run into the Darklings before Gaius returns with Merlin's Crystal. And without the crystal, Leftie will probably kill us on sight –

especially if he finds out Camelot broke the treaty and imprisoned a Darkling crow.'

She puffed out her cheeks in frustration. 'And even it we don't run into him, we might end up someplace worse, like the Saxon camp!'

Calib sniffed the air, trying to catch a hint of water, but it was hard when the cold made his nose runny.

'We should head west,' he finally said. 'Away from the mountains. We know Leftie's lair is hidden in its foothills, so the farther away we get from them, the better.'

Cecily nodded, and they began to distance themselves from the row of jagged peaks rising in the east like the teeth of a great sea monster.

They trudged in silence, not daring to breathe a word. From time to time, they doubled back on their tracks, just in case more weasels were still prowling about the woods.

As they travelled, worries crawled around Calib's head like hungry fire ants. Even though it felt like a lifetime ago, they had only left Camelot yesterday morning. Calib wondered whether Kensington's war party had reached the Darklings by now.

'You know, they're going to think we were kidnapped,' Cecily said, as if reading Calib's mind.

'Or that we're traitors,' Calib added. They fell back into silence. Calib could feel every muscle ache, like he'd gone twenty rounds against the Hurler.

Eventually, they heard the reassuring burbling of the river again. Cecily waded into an eddy to wash off some of the fish stench. Calib knelt down to splash icy water on his face. His stomach growled. He hoped General Gaius would come back for them soon. Without Merlin's Crystal, they had nothing to bargain with.

'Who do you think that weasel meant by the Manderlean?' Calib asked as Cecily used some twigs and her cloak to create a temporary tent over a pile of brown leaves. The name sounded familiar, but he couldn't place it – like a nightmare that he'd forgotten upon waking.

'It sounded as if the Manderlean was their leader,' Cecily said, burrowing into the leaf pile. 'Whoever – or whatever – that is.'

Calib nodded. He would remember the name and ask Sir Alric when they got back to the castle. Sir Alric often pored through the library scrolls, seeking inspiration for new contraptions. He was easily Camelot's most knowledgeable mouse.

Calib used his own cloak for a tent and covered himself with some leaves too. Settling in to wait for the great horned owl, he let his eyelids grow heavy.

His dreams carried him back to Camelot. He was standing in the tapestry hall again, staring at his parents' tapestry. His father still offered Merlin's Crystal, glowing with bright blue flames.

When beliefs as old as stone will budge, then minds as sharp as swords will be free, Sir Trenton said in Howell's voice.

Calib woke with a start. His heart and head were pounding. He sat straight up, fur prickling. Something was moving towards them.

That thought had barely formed when his tent was suddenly whipped aside. A squirrel in a black hood stared at him with triumphant eyes.

'Got 'em, boys!' he shouted to the other masked squirrels behind him.

Before Calib could cry for help, the intruder grabbed a hold of his ear and dragged him out of the leaf pile. His other arm grabbed a sleeping Cecily.

A net was thrown over the both of them. Calib counted three masked and hooded black squirrels standing around them with bows and arrows drawn.

Darkling scouts.

Two more descended from the trees above on ropes of ivy.

'Wait! We're not enemies!' Calib cried.

'Funny,' one of the hooded squirrels growled. 'You smell like our stolen food. And if my ears don't lie, you sound like a pair of Camelot mice!'

'We didn't take your food! You've made a mistake!' Calib struggled to get out of the netting, but the thick rope was heavy, and the knots were tied tight.

'Leftie's orders are to capture first, ask questions later.'

Quick as lightning, Cecily took out her sword and slashed at the rope, breaking apart the net. She struggled to pull Calib out after her.

'That one is escaping!' said one of their attackers.

A rock flew at Cecily from the trees.

'Watch out!' Calib shouted. It hit the side of Cecily's head, twisting her around. She dropped her sword in surprise and fell heavily on the river-bank. She began sliding towards the water.

'Cecily!' Calib ran forward, but he was still tangled in the net. Every part of his body went numb as he struggled to get to his friend.

'Victory!' A bloodcurdling screech echoed from above them.

Out of nowhere, General Gaius swooped in, grabbing Cecily before she hit the water. A volley of arrows came at the general, but he swerved out of the way. Banking hard, he started to turn around, doubling back for Calib.

'Just get Cecily to safety!' Calib shouted.

General Gaius nodded once and took off into the trees. He narrowly avoided the second round of arrows that whizzed by his wings.

Rough arms closed in around Calib's body, and he felt something hit his head from behind. As his vision faded to darkness, the last thing he saw was Merlin's Crystal dangling from General Gaius's neck as the owl carried Cecily's limp body into the sky.

Chapter Thirty

Calib awoke in a dark cavern lit by oily torches. The air smelled of dry leaves and singed feathers. He sat up, every muscle protesting as he did. The back of his head pulsed from where a squirrel had hit him.

How long have I been out? Calib wondered. *How long until the Camelot army arrives with their war cries?*

As Calib's eyes adjusted to the dim surroundings, he noticed gleaming eyes staring back at him. Every manner of Darkling creature – from crows to foxes, hares to squirrels – stood watching him just outside the light's glow. The cave was packed and stuffy, and the sound of shuffling paws and rustling feathers echoed off the walls.

A black crow stepped forward. His feathers were painted with green-and-red battle stripes.

'Leftie, he wakes!' the crow squawked, addressing someone behind Calib. With a trembling belly full of fear, Calib turned.

A fearsome lynx towered over him. The big cats were rare in this part of the world, and Leftie was by far the most fearsome of the few who still lived in Britain. His fur was a matted and mangy yellow. A patch covered the place where his right eye used to be. Thin red scars poked out from underneath the cloth. He was dressed in a kilt made of fur pelts, and on his paws, he wore rings decorated with short blades.

Leftie grinned widely, displaying every one of his finely sharpened fangs.

'My, my, look at what my squirrels have brought me,' Leftie hissed in Calib's face. 'A lost little Camelot mousie.'

The animals in the cave cackled.

'How much do ye reckon Camelot will pay to get one of their little 'uns back?' Leftie said, appraising Calib with his one good eye. 'Too bad the other 'un got away; could have doubled our price!'

Calib thought of Cecily. Hot, angry tears welled in his eyes. He prayed that General Gaius was able to get her to safety.

'We're here trying to save you, trying to *warn* you, and you tried to kill us instead!' Calib burst out. 'My friend could be . . . She might be . . .' Calib didn't dare to finish his sentence. He felt light-headed from anger and fear.

'My squirrels did exactly as they were ordered. In this forest, we cannot have our enemies prancing about in our backyard like fairies,' Leftie said. His eye narrowed, and the smile had left his face. 'These are dangerous days, and we do what we must to survive.'

'And I suppose it doesn't matter that you hurt innocent creatures in the process?' Calib shouted.

'Spare me your righteousness!' Leftie unsheathed a scimitar and hooked Calib's neck with it, forcing the mouse to stand on tiptoes to keep the blade from digging into his skin. 'It is *precisely* the innocent I'm trying to protect! But I suppose all Darklings are villains to you. I should cut your mousey throat for everyone in this good company to see.'

The metal pressed against his fur, and a few strands of fur hair floated down, severed by the sharp blade. Calib focused his terror on everything that was at stake: it wasn't just his life or Cecily's life hanging in the balance, but the lives of all at Camelot. If he pushed Leftie too far, it would do more harm than good. Calib needed the lynx to listen to him. He hadn't come this far to be killed by an overgrown housecat.

'What grows strong when the strong grow weak?' Calib croaked out.

Leftie paused. His one good eye blinked a few times.

'What did you just say?' He didn't release Calib, but the scimitar trembled slightly in his paws.

'I won Merlin's Crystal from the owls,' he whispered. 'We were bringing it to you, but you decided to attack us instead.'

'It's a useless piece of rock!' Leftie spat. 'Obviously, the crystal didn't give any "great strength" to the owls, as they were unable to defeat us in the the Fellwater Swamps and had to flee!'

Calib's fear, which he'd been trying to hold back, now flooded his entire body. If Leftie didn't want Merlin's Crystal any more, he had no way to bargain for his life or for peace. He began to shake.

Seeing this, Leftie sneered. 'What makes you think I wanted that pebble in the first place?'

Act like a Christopher!

Calib drew himself up to his full three inches. 'Valentina Stormbeak told us you did on the night I helped her escape from Camelot!'

At this, concerned chatter broke out among the crows.

'You must think I'm some newborn kitten,' the lynx snarled. 'Valentina has not been heard from in three days. She was flying south to bring her clan to the fold. She was supposed to return yesterday. For all we know, she could be in your dungeon right now.'

Calib's stomach did a double flip. Had Valentina been recaptured?

Leftie released him roughly. 'Council, what do you say? Do we spare the prisoner, or do we dispose of him?'

A handful of woodland creatures came forward into the light, forming a half-circle around Calib. The mouse guessed from their markings and clothes that these were the leaders of the various Darkling tribes. There was a fierce female fox, a vixen with rusty red fur. Much of it was streaked with green-and-brown paint, as if to camouflage her colours better. A hare wore a long coat of copper chain mail, and his ears were decorated with a row of spiky hoops. A badger's head nearly touched the cavern ceiling. On his front, he wore a tortoise shell as a breastplate.

'I say we kill this one,' a black squirrel declared, 'and send those Camelot scum a message.'

'You don't understand!' Calib piped up, desperate to turn the tide in his favour. 'The Saxons and their weasels are here. They're invading again. And I have reason to believe they killed my grandfather, Commander Yvers! Please, you just have to *listen*.'

'Yvers murdered, eh?' Leftie's voice was emotionless, but his eyes flickered with surprise. 'It was only a matter of time before the old fur ball got what was coming to him.'

'Yvers was the greatest commander who ever lived!' Calib lashed out again.

'Quiet, mouse,' Leftie said. 'Or we will gag you with your tail. Master Jans Thropper, your thoughts?'

'It's not worth the risk to keep him alive,' the hare said, the hoops in his ears clinking together. The badger in the tortoise-shell armour gave a low growl in agreement.

'The mouse-knights would have us bear the brunt

of the attacks while they wait behind their high and mighty walls,' the fox added.

'Who knows what secrets this one has already gleaned as a spy,' the badger said.

'Quite right, Master Lylas Whitestripe,' Leftie said, nodding to the badger.

'Perhaps we're being hasty,' the vixen said doubtfully. 'I knew Commander Yvers to be a decent beast.'

'Aye, and his grandson is a fine one as well,' a voice spoke up from outside the circle. 'So paws off that mouse!'

Chapter Thirty-One

'Valentina!' Calib bolted straight for the weary-looking crow, and they shared a fur-and-feather hug.

'Hello, Master Calib,' Valentina said with a quick affectionate nibble of his ear.

'*Now* do you believe me?' Calib said, turning to the lynx.

'What Calib says is true,' Valentina said. 'He helped me – at great risk to himself – when Camelot accused us of Commander Yvers's murder.' Valentina bobbed her head at Calib. 'I did not think you would truly pay us a visit, however. You are very brave, Calib. Very brave or very stupid.'

Leftie scrutinised Calib and Valentina. Behind them, a host of new crows was filing into the cavern. Space was becoming tight, and the tension among the Darklings seemed to grow with it.

'This cave is getting too crowded,' the fox said to Leftie in a low voice. 'I mean no disrespect. But we simply don't have enough food for everyone. Not if you continue taking in refugees.'

'I will not turn away any beast to face the winter alone, even it means we all go a little lean,' Leftie said.

'"A little lean"?' Llyas said, shaking his head so that his tortoise-shells clicked together. 'We'll starve to death!'

Calib thought of all the animals stuck in this cave, living off mere scraps, and he remembered the ample amount of food in Camelot's cellars. The dried, salted fish and drying herbs, the barrels full of oats and barley, and the drams of dandelion and elderberry cordial. It just didn't seem right that the Darklings should starve because they happened to live in the woods.

'Camelot needs more defenders, and you need more food,' Calib said hurriedly, before he could change his mind. 'If the Saxons rise against us, none of us will be safe. We could work together.'

The silence that followed this outburst was absolute. The Darklings looked at Calib as if he'd offered a share of lost treasure. For a long time, no one spoke.

'If Camelot promises us food and shelter, that's where I vote we go,' Valentina said. 'Anyone who lets pride get in the way of providing for their clan . . . Well, that's no leader at all.'

'All I know is that the little ones are hungry,' said a ragged-looking squirrel.

'Or we could attack the castle ourselves and *take* the food!' Lylas the badger bared his teeth in a mean smile.

'And you think we have the might to mount that kind of attack?' a crow asked. 'We're barely able to protect what little food we have left. We have no fighters to spare.'

More arguments broke out: crows squawked and badgers grumbled and squirrels chattered shrilly at one another. Calib resisted the urge to cover his ears with his hands. It was as if he was in the council room at Camelot all over again. Calib recalled how many times Commander Yvers had worked to unify the various animals at Camelot. Whether it was forging an alliance with the moat otters or listening to the endless complaints from

the bell tower larks, Commander Yvers had always known how to restore order.

Calib yearned for his grandfather's kindness and patience, the way he'd found Calib in the tapestry hall on the very day he was too afraid to compete in the Harvest Tournament. How long ago that seemed.

Spotting a little outcropping of rock that formed a platform, Calib leaped nimbly on top of it. He cleared his throat.

'Can I have your attention, please?' he shouted above the din. No one even looked at him.

He cupped his paws to his mouth and tried again.

'PLEASE, CAN I HAVE YOUR ATTENTION!' Calib shouted again at the top of his lungs.

As the Darkling leaders finally quieted, they turned to Calib, surprised that such a loud voice could come from such a small mouse. But with all eyes on him now, Calib's confidence seemed to shrink back into a tiny ball.

'I have no right to tell you what to do,' Calib said, addressing the crowd in a squeak. He wished he had Commander Yvers's deep, soothing voice – but wishing, he knew, would not solve anything. He was a small mouse with ragged ears, and a squeak of a voice, but he would have to be enough. 'Camelot has a motto: "Together in paw and tail, lest divided we fall and fail." That applies to you, our Darkling friends, as well.'

Leftie looked at him, weighing his next words carefully.

'Since you are so eager to share your opinion,' he said. 'How do you plan to put paw and tail together, as you say?'

Calib took a deep breath. At least Leftie was listening to him.

'First, we need to clear Two-Bits's name,' Calib said.

'Two-Bits?!' Leftie let out a big guffaw. 'What's poor Two-Bits got to do with it?'

'Two-Bits's tooth has been used as evidence of his role in killing my grandfather,' Calib explained. 'Sir Percival said he found it on Commander Yvers when he was examining the body.'

Leftie gawked at him. 'Why, that big baby couldn't hurt a fly! The answer to your mystery is solved easily enough: he had his tooth removed just last week. In fact, your healer, Sir Percival, pulled it for him. Two-Bits?'

Calib felt as if he'd been doused by ice water as the black squirrel stepped forward reluctantly. His

222

jaw was still bandaged together. He looked like he had just woken up from a nap.

'Poor thing's been chewing poppies to numb the pain,' Leftie said. 'He's had to hibernate early.'

Calib felt the ground spinning beneath him. He closed his eyes, steadying himself on the cavern wall. Of course. The traitor in Camelot.

'Sir Percival Vole!' Calib said in a harsh whisper, piecing everything together. 'Sir Percival has been framing Two-Bits as Commander Yvers's murderer. He must have convinced Warren to lie . . .'

But why would Sir Percival, a Knight of the Round Table, do such a thing?

'Typical Camelot behaviour,' scoffed Jans Thropper. 'And we're supposed to believe this scruff of fur when he says he wants to help us?'

Calib ignored that.

'We have to clear Two-Bits,' Calib repeated loudly, trying to focus even as his mind still reeled. 'We have to send a message back to Camelot. There's enough food for everyone, and safety behind its walls. We just have to clear your name.'

If he could get Leftie and Two-Bits to talk to Commander Kensington and convince her, then the Camelot mice would see they had been wrong all along about the Darklings. They would see they had no choice but to join forces against the returning Saxons.

Leftie hesitated. Calib held his breath.

In the silence, a far-off horn sounded a short staccato melody.

Leftie and his lieutenants immediately bolted up from their seats. Lylas growled – a low rumbling that vibrated through the room. The fox let out an earsplitting yowl that made Calib stumble back. Two of the Darkling crows sprang forward and grabbed Calib's arms with their beaks, wrenching them behind his back.

'We should have known this was all a trick!' The fox bared her teeth at Calib. The fur on her neck bristled.

'Quickly! Get everyone to safety!' Leftie barked. 'Retrieve your weapons!'

'What?' Calib was confused – What had happened? Why was everyone panicking?

The lynx turned on Calib, and his eye was full of contempt. 'T'was the alarm for Camelot invaders,' he hissed, whipping out his sharp, bladed rings. 'Your patrols are here.'

Chapter Thirty-Two

An arrow whizzed across the cavern. It missed Leftie's head by inches before bouncing off the cave wall behind the lynx.

'It's a setup!' shouted Thropper, whipping out his fighting staff.

Just then, Commander Kensington, flanked by Sir Owen and Sir Percival, appeared in the cave's mouth.

'Charrrrge!' Commander Kensington yelled, pointing her sword. A line of Camelot soldiers filed into the cave behind her, swords drawn.

'Time to flush some Darkling pests out of their

nests!' cried Sir Owen. He unsheathed his double daggers.

Caught by surprise, the Darklings swarmed forward. Fighters dashed to meet the Camelot soldiers while the young and old animals clamoured over one another, trying to escape farther into the caves and tunnels.

Leftie turned back to Calib. 'To think we listened to you for even a second!' Leftie bared his fangs. 'I should have known that Camelot would resort to dirty tricks.' He drew out his scimitar and stepped towards Calib. The mouse backed up against the cave wall. Calib knew now that it was too late. There were no more words that could stop what would come next. He closed his eyes and thought of his mother, father, and grandfather. Would they be waiting for him in the Fields Beyond, to welcome him with open arms?

Would they be disappointed in him?

'Leftie Wildfang!' Kensington roared. Suddenly, she was there, brandishing her broadsword at the feline. 'The Darklings are charged with the murder of our commander! Surrender and call off your fighters!'

'Over my fur pelt!' snarled Leftie, twisting

around. He lunged at Commander Kensington with a snap of his teeth.

The lynx was alarmingly fast for a creature his size – but Kensington was faster.

She darted between Leftie's legs, her broadsword a blur of steel as she slashed left and right, trying to penetrate his thick fur. Leftie yowled as one blow found flesh, and he swiped a massive paw in the direction of the mouse-sized whirlwind. Kensington ducked as Leftie's claws grazed her armour, and then she redoubled her attack. The sound of clashing metal echoed through the cave.

'Stop! You're fighting the wrong enemy!' Calib shouted over the chaos. Yelps and growls filled the air, drowning out his pleas. The fox swung out her stick, slamming three Camelot mice to the cave wall. The crows were struggling to cast off nets that had been thrown over them. Lylas the badger was taking on at least six different mice, snarling and foaming at the mouth.

Calib looked on helplessly, shouting his voice raw though he knew it would do no good. All his hard work had been dashed to pieces in a matter of seconds.

'Into the tunnels, Darklings!' Leftie shouted, breaking away from Commander Kensington. At the lynx's command, the Darklings retreated deeper into the cave. Sensing an upper paw, Commander Kensington urged the Camelot troops forward. Bounding to a higher ledge, Leftie threw his weight against the stone wall.

A great rumbling reverberated through the cavern.

Looking up, Calib saw that the rock Leftie had moved had caused a chain reaction, loosening a pile of stones on a ledge right above their heads. All at once, the rocks began crashing down around them.

'The cave is collapsing!' Commander Kensington shouted to her soldiers. 'Flee!'

Calib had little choice but to follow the Camelot fighters. The mice ran for the cave's mouth while pebbles rained down around them.

As they burst into sunlight, a great thundering sounded from behind. An avalanche of stone and rubble filled the space that had been the Darkling cave, discharging a great cloud of dust into the air.

As Calib stood gasping and brushing debris from his fur, he felt something grab his ear from behind and yank up. He found himself looking into the beady, calculating eyes of Sir Percival.

'Looks like we found our Darkling traitor after all,' he said, barely hiding an oily smirk.

Sir Owen was staring at Calib, shock written all over his face. His one whisker twitched agitatedly. 'Calib Christopher! How could you, laddie? Conspiring with the enemy! Turning your back on your own kind?'

Before Calib could respond, Sir Percival threw Calib backwards, into the hands of waiting soldiers. 'We'll interrogate him properly when we are back at Camelot. For now, take this traitor to the dungeons.'

Chapter Thirty-Three

Sir Kay squinted at the tattered note Galahad had retrieved from the lark. Galahad, Malcolm, and Bors stood at attention, waiting to serve high tea to the queen and the castle's steward. There should have been more knights to wait upon, but only Sir Kay had heeded the queen's call to the council.

'I don't see what you are going on about,' Sir Kay said, shrugging and passing the note back to the queen. 'This is clearly a routine update. Why are you wasting our time with these senseless meetings?'

'Truly, you cannot be so blind as that,' Queen

Guinevere said, her green eyes flashing. 'What other interpretation of "danger", "rumours" and "prepare" could there be? It bears the names of the knights who patrol the Iron Mountains. They would be the first to send warning. What further proof do you need that something is happening?'

Sir Kay put on his thick spectacles to study the message closer.

'I'm fairly certain this blur before "danger" is a "no". As in "no danger". And this –' he pointed to another ink smear – 'is "just". As in, "just rumours".'

Galahad clenched the edges of his serving platter as he stepped forward with mugs of hot cider. He resisted the urge to dump the drinks over Sir Kay's head. Beside him, he could see Bors roll his eyes as he pushed the pastry cart forward.

'All right, I will not speak of warnings again,' Guinevere said. There was a certain steeliness to her words, but she kept her voice even and diplomatic. 'However, I see no harm in putting extra sentries on the wall as a precaution.'

Sir Kay nearly sputtered into his mug. 'My dear queen, we knights have fought and bled for Camelot so that we could enjoy some peace and quiet. I shall not disturb any knight's well-earned rest with womanly panic!'

'Then our conversation here is done,' Guinevere said, standing up. 'You may leave. Now.'

Galahad could see Sir Kay was taken aback by the queen's sharp dismissal. But after a second, he only shrugged, stuffing a berry scone and a flaky pastry into his cloak's pocket. He bowed stiffly towards the queen and then left.

Galahad and Bors looked at each other, unsure of what to do. The queen held her head in her hands and rubbed her temples.

'Your Majesty?' Galahad asked tentatively. 'Are we also dismissed?'

'They would never dare to speak to Arthur in such a way,' she said, not hearing Galahad. Her shoulders were slumped, and it seemed to him as though Queen Guinevere was holding all the stones of the castle on her back. And in a way . . . she was.

'Your Majesty,' Galahad said again, 'There must be something *we* can do. Even if we aren't knights.'

'Yes,' said someone from behind him. Galahad turned in surprise. It was Malcolm who had spoken – Malcolm who didn't offer to do anything unless it benefited him. Galahad peered closely at him, looking for a smirk or gleam that hinted at incoming trouble. But to Galahad's surprise, there was no trace of laughter on the older page's face.

'What if *we*, the pages, stand watch on the wall instead, Your Majesty?' Malcolm continued.

'That might do,' the queen said, studying them thoughtfully.

'My older brother is lord of a small holding near the Iron Mountains. He sent the message,' said Malcolm, worry creasing his large brow. 'And I know he would not waste a lark if there was no news to report.'

'I can take the first watch tonight,' Bors volunteered.

Guinevere looked at the three young pages standing before her with a ghost of a smile.

'They underestimate you as much as they underestimate our enemies,' Guinevere said. 'My new defenders of Camelot. Much will be asked of you in the dark times ahead. But if you keep your eyes open and work together as brothers, we may stand a chance.'

Malcolm, Galahad, and Bors nodded. No one mentioned that this was the first time all three of them had ever agreed on anything.

Chapter Thirty-Four

The door to Valentina's former cage clicked shut behind Calib. The hinges had been fixed, and a stronger padlock had been added to the door to make escape impossible.

'Keep a constant eye on the prisoner, Warren,' Sir Percival instructed the page with his usual, black-toothed smile. Both Sir Percival and Warren had escorted him promptly to the dungeon when they arrived back in Camelot. 'Perhaps after he's had some time to reflect on his actions, he would like to make a confession. And remember, Warren, this could be *you* if you don't follow my instructions.'

Warren saluted Sir Percival, but Calib noticed his paw was trembling. He must have known, of course, that Calib wasn't the true traitor.

'Stop lying, Sir Percival!' Calib said, rubbing his wrists to get blood back into them. 'I know you're helping the Saxons!'

Sir Percival gave him a look of mock pity, barely concealing the malice behind his eyes. 'Such a shame that the Christopher legacy should end in such an ignoble way,' he said, walking back out of the cellars. 'I don't imagine *you'll* be on any tapestries.'

Warren stationed himself facing the cage, looking anywhere but directly at Calib. Fury crackled through Calib like a tinder spark set to dry kindling.

'Why?' Calib demanded of the grey mouse. '*Why* are you helping Sir Percival? You *know* you didn't see a black squirrel kill Grandfather! Why are you lying?'

'I'm *not* lying!' Warren said hotly, but Calib saw his eyes dart towards the door. 'So what if I didn't see the squirrel myself? Sir Percival saw Two-Bits. What does it matter if I told Commander Kensington that fact or if Sir Percival did? Either way, that Darkling was there! Two-Bits killed Commander Yvers!'

Suddenly, it all made sense to Calib. Warren had agreed to tell Commander Kensington that he had seen the squirrel because he had hoped it would put him in good standing with the commander. Maybe he had even thought that the famous knight would ask him to be her personal squire after he passed the Harvest Tournament. It was a prestigious position, and one that would surely help Warren achieve knighthood himself.

To his dismay, Calib found that he could empathise with the grey mouse. He knew all too well the burning desire to become a knight of Camelot.

Warren's ribs heaved, as if he had been running laps around the training arena. Looking at the way his fur was now glossy with sweat, Calib thought that there might still be a chance to convince Warren to tell the truth.

'Warren, listen – you must tell Commander Kensington that *you* didn't actually see Two-Bits!' Calib said, his words urgent. 'If you tell the truth, they might give me a chance to explain! Be brave,' he pushed. 'It's what a knight would do.'

Warren met his eyes, and for a second, Calib thought Warren was going to say yes. But then the grey mouse dropped his gaze.

'I can't,' he whispered. 'What if Commander

Kensington won't let me become a squire? And besides, if you're right, Sir Percival would – He would – '

It seemed as though his fear of Sir Percival had clamped Warren's mouth shut. He turned his back on Calib and stared at the door.

Calib's fury fizzled out into despair, twisting up like a lump of coal in his chest.

'If you won't tell the truth,' he pleaded, 'then just tell me: is Cecily all right?'

Warren remained unresponsive, refusing to acknowledge Calib for the rest of the evening.

The night dragged on. Being underground, Calib could not tell how much time had passed. With no one coming to visit, and no one willing to deliver news or food, Calib lay back on the dirty sock he was supposed to use for a bed mat. It still reeked of human feet, and he was nauseated.

He stayed awake long into the night. Warren's snoring would have been too loud to ignore even if Calib's anxious thoughts had allowed him to sleep. As it was, he could not stop thinking about what had happened. Over and over again, he was rooted to the ground, watching Cecily get hit and crumple. Over and over again, he saw the large shadow attack his grandfather. His failures felt like stones in his stomach. Calib brushed away the tears that dampened his fur.

'Calib?' a soft voice whispered his name.

A silhouette appeared, just out of the flickering light. Calib rose to his feet. 'Who's there?'

'Shh!' The silhouette stepped forward. It was Ginny, Cecily's best friend, looking anxious as ever, with a small stack of tea sandwiches made from bread crusts and cucumber peels. 'I wanted to come as soon as I'd heard you were back, but I had to wait until everyone would be sleeping. These are for you,' she said, slipping the food between the bars.

'Thank you,' Calib whispered, and even though it had been hours since he had last eaten, he wasn't the least bit hungry.

'How is Cecily? Is she . . .' Calib paused as he prayed the answer wasn't his worst nightmare come true, 'all right?'

Ginny's face fell. 'Not really,' she said, her voice catching with emotion. 'She's had a terrible fever all evening. Sir Alric is watching over her while Sir Percival has gone off to gather herbs for medicine.'

At the mention of Sir Percival, Calib's anger filled him like a flood.

'Don't trust him, Ginny,' Calib warned. 'Sir

Percival is the one who's been lying to us all along about the Darklings.'

'Shush!' Ginny reached through the bars and clapped a paw over Calib's mouth as Warren stirred. They waited a few breathless moments, and then Warren began to snore again. Calib backed away from Ginny's paw.

'What's going to happen to me?' Calib asked.

'I don't know,' she said honestly. 'The knights are meeting in the morning to discuss it, along with planning the next offensive attack on the Darklings.' Then her ears perked up. 'But I did have one funny bit of news. It seems that one of the Two-Leggers has been trying to talk to us.'

'What do you mean?' Calib's pulse quickened.

'Barnaby found a message, written in bread crumbs, placed in front of the tunnel that leads into the throne room.'

Calib latched on to this bit of news like a lifeline. 'What did the message say?'

'That's the funny thing,' Ginny said. 'It just said "thank you". Have you ever heard of such a thing? I wonder if the first-year pages are just trying to play a trick on us.'

But before Calib could inquire further, Warren stirred again.

'I better go.' Ginny gave Calib's paw one last squeeze and then scurried away.

Stinging thoughts darted around in Calib's head. If only there was a way to get Galahad back into the cellar again . . .

If only he'd reached the Darklings more quickly . . .

If only . . .

Just as Calib was about to drift off, a horn sounded in the distance.

Warren bolted upright. Moments later the sound of thudding pawsteps approached the entrance to the room.

'Warren, to the walls!' barked Sir Alric, who appeared in full armour at the doorway. 'The Darklings have been spotted outside the borders! All pages need to fill in for the sentries!'

'Wait! What about me?' Calib called, but Warren was already scrambling up the stairs after Sir Alric. There was a moment of silence, and then Calib thought he heard muffled pawsteps. Had they come back for him?

Calib held his breath, waiting, but no one entered the room. And yet . . . suddenly, a strange certainty filled Calib: someone was watching him. He turned towards the corner, away from the door, and saw a pair of eyes peer out at him from the other side of the cage.

A dark, wet nose appeared between the bars, followed by a pair of unmistakable mismatched eyes.

'Howell?' Calib whispered.

The wolf seemed to glow faintly, even though there was no moonlight to reflect in the dank cellar dungeon. More remarkable still, Howell looked translucent.

'You are quite popular this evening, Calib Christopher,' the wolf said. 'It's been difficult to speak with you privately.'

'How do you do that?' Calib asked, breathless with amazement. '*Who* are you?'

'I go by many names,' Howell answered, a sharp-toothed grin spreading across his face. 'Howell, Myrddin, Emrys . . . Merlin.'

Calib's jaw dropped. *Howell* was the famous Two-Legger wizard? Was it possible?. All this time, Calib had been speaking to the greatest wizard the world had ever known. He suddenly felt shy. And yet . . . something occurred to him.

'It was you,' the mouse said breathlessly. 'You put the Sword in the Stone, didn't you?'

'Goodness, no.' Howell shook his head. 'The

Darkling Woods possess secret ways of warning, my dear mouse. The Sword in the Stone is an older and wilder kind of magic than any I command. All I can do is interpret what signs are left of it in this world.'

Calib remembered the tales of the old days, when magical beings like fairies, elves, and giants lived among other animals in peace.

'I need your help, Calib,' Howell said sombrely.

Calib blinked at him, certain he'd misheard.

'"Help"?' Calib repeated. 'You're the greatest wizard who ever lived. I'm just a mouse. How can I possibly help you?'

Howell sighed.

'My powers have diminished as the magic of this world has waned. I've preserved what magic I can by living as a wolf. I am of no more use to men, and I have only one last spell in me. I will free you from this place. You must do the rest.'

'But why spend your last spell freeing me?' Calib asked. 'I've already *failed*! I'm useless! Because of me, the Darklings are marching on Camelot even now!'

'You are your father's son,' Howell said sternly. 'It is a resemblance not in your whisker length or fur colouring. The power is inside of you; you just have to learn to listen. Give me your paw, Calib Christopher.'

Calib obliged, slipping his paws through the bars. The wolf laid his enormous paw gently on Calib's trembling one.

'*Resera*,' he said. His voice seemed to come from far away. Howell began to fade before Calib's eyes. The outline of his wolf shape blurred.

'Both the Darkling and the Saxon armies are attacking this very morning,' Howell continued. Now he was no more than a hovering ball of fading light. 'Only when all of Camelot's creatures have been united will you be able to defeat the Manderlean.'

For a long moment, all Calib could see was darkness. And in that darkness, Merlin's voice echoed, frail and distant.

'I have no more power in this world. My magic is spent. *You* must help them now.'

A flash of brilliant blue light blinded Calib. Slowly, the edges of his vision filled in like the grey of twilight. A blast of cold winter wind made his whiskers twitch. He suddenly felt the cool damp of earth and grass beneath his paws.

His cage was gone, along with the dank dungeon beyond it. Calib stood on top of a hill, about a league from the castle, with a clear view of an open meadow beneath a sky still flecked with fading stars. On the horizon, a rosy-pink light promised that dawn was not far behind.

'Where are we, Merlin?' he asked in amazement. But there was no reply.

Calib looked around, expecting to see the human wizard, or perhaps Howell the wolf, but there was no one else. He was alone, and in the distance, he could hear a trumpet sound the charge.

A battle was beginning.

Chapter Thirty-Five

The first rays of sun fell across the open ground, illuminating the Camelot troops marching across it. Little red banners dotted the landscape, signalling the position of various regiments. Beyond the meadow, between the bare branches of a nearby grove, Calib could see a great confusion of movement.

Black birds beat the air with their wings. Smaller, blurred figures leaped among the lower branches. Calib could make out a large, tawny shape lunging between the tree trunks with feline grace. It could only be Leftie the lynx, sunlight glinting off his armour.

Calib dashed down the side of the hill as fast as his paws would carry him. He threw himself into the tall grass, making a beeline for the grove. He didn't know how he could stop the battle, but he knew he had to try.

Merlin trusted him. But how – how was he supposed to help?

The ground was slippery with frost. Short tufts of grass crackled icily beneath his paws. It was hard going across the uneven ground, clambering over furrows and worming his way through brambles. He was soon out of breath. But he hardly noticed.

His mind was racing. Help, help, help. How could he help?

Approaching an embankment, Calib found his way blocked by a Two-Legger stone wall. It wasn't very high, but it was well built, with mortar between the stones. He ran along the base, searching frantically for a way through it, but there were no openings large enough to admit a mouse. The only way was over.

He dragged himself up from stone to stone, pawhold to pawhold. His muscles were already tired from his sprint, and the rock was slick with ice, unyielding beneath his paws. Once, he lost his grip and almost went tumbling down to the ground, but he managed to cling precariously to a patch of lichen until he regained his footing. At last, gasping and panting, he pulled himself onto the top of the wall.

A flash of movement at the southeast edge of the forest caught Calib's eye. At first he thought he had imagined it, but as he stared across the meadow, he saw something – or some*things* – emerging from the southeast.

His heart stopped.

A mass of moving creatures spilled from the forest, spreading out along the tree line as more and more of them poured out into the meadow.

Saxon weasels.

Calib could see them from the wall. But they were visible for only half a dozen feet beyond the border of the forest before disappearing into the tall meadow grass. After that, the only sign of the creatures was the violent swaying of the grass that marked their snaky path to the castle . . . and towards the unsuspecting, warring mice and Darklings fighting in the grove ahead.

Calib would never be able to warn the Camelot army in time – He was too slow! There was simply

247

no way for him to reach the grove before the animals were ambushed. He was paralysed. Why had Merlin placed so much trust in him? He was only a mouse, after all – and not even a very *capable* one.

A raucous cawing suddenly filled the air around him.

Calib instinctively ducked as a flock of crows whizzed overhead, flying low to the ground, their shadows skating over the frozen grass.

'Wait!' Calib yelled up at them. 'Come back! The Saxons are attacking!'

But either the birds hadn't heard him, or else they were too focused on the ongoing melee between Camelot and the Darklings to care about one little mouse.

Calib jumped and hollered, waving his arms and shouting at them to come back. But by now, they were too far away to hear him.

'I'll give you this much, Calib Christopher,' said a familiar voice. 'You're a mouse who knows how to find trouble.'

'Valentina!' Calib's hopes lifted as the crow circled and then alighted on the wall.

'Looks like you're late for the battle too,' she said.

'Can you take me there?' Calib said eagerly.

The crow hesitated. 'And if I did, which side would you be fighting on?'

Calib groaned in frustration. 'We're all on the same side. That's what I've been telling you. Look!'

He pointed towards the meadow. The flood of weasels from the Darkling Woods had finally ceased, but the long grass was a seething torrent of motion. In places the grass had been trampled flat, and Calib could see a steady stream of long, sinuous bodies clad in armour.

Valentina froze. 'By beak and talon,' she whispered in shock. 'How many are there?'

'Too many! We have to warn everyone, before *both* our forces are overrun!'

Valentina nodded. 'Right. Grab on and hold tight.' She held out one leg to Calib, and he climbed carefully onto her foot and balanced himself between her narrow toes.

With a quick hop, Valentina launched herself off the wall and into the air. The world spun crazily beneath Calib. He gave a yelp of fright. This was nothing like riding in the basket that General Gaius had carried. Then, he and Cecily had been sheltered from the wind and the dizzying view. Now there was nothing but sleek black feathers above him and the unforgiving ground below.

In almost no time they were past the Saxon vanguard. And shortly after that, they were in the grove, dodging between the branches of scrubby trees. Calib's heart leaped and plunged with every dip of Valentina's wings. Calib could see Darkling and Camelot creatures fighting all around. Here, a band of Darkling archers had a troop of shrews pinned down behind a boulder. There, three of the moat otters had a badger surrounded, though a group of hares were coming to her aid. In the canopy around them, crows and larks swooped and dived, feathers flying as they locked talons in combat.

'Stop fighting! The Saxons are attacking!' Calib shouted as Valentina flew low over the battle.

'Regroup!' Valentina cawed. 'Weasels on the southeast flank!'

But no one paid them any attention.

A flurry of fur and steel caught Calib's eye – Leftie, crouched on a fallen log, exchanging vicious blows with Commander Kensington and Sir Owen.

Valentina flew straight for the log and pulled up sharply in front of Leftie and the knights, flapping her wings wildly to get their attention. Calib let go of her leg and rolled to a hard landing in the dirt. He looked up to see all three combatants staring down at him, mouths agape.

'Calib Christopher?' Kensington's voice was equal parts anger and disbelief.

'Commander! Leftie!' he burst out. 'You need to stop the battle – We're about to be ambushed!'

Leftie bared his teeth at Calib. 'Is this another Camelot deception?'

'I swear it!' Calib shouted. 'We're all in terrible danger!'

'Stop your nonsense, Calib,' Kensington said. 'Who do you pretend is going to ambush us?'

Calib looked up at Valentina for support.

'Them,' Valentina said in a hoarse whisper, and Calib turned to see a writhing tide of weasels emerge from the grass, advancing towards them like a dark wave from a stormy sea – endless and unstoppable.

Chapter Thirty-Six

The predawn air was still, like the eerie calm before a storm, as Galahad stepped onto Camelot's ramparts. He watched his breath come out in white gusts, and felt the bitter chill seep into his woollen clothes.

In the nunnery, they called weather like this the Silent Sleep. With no wind to speak of, unseasoned travellers sometimes were tricked into believing it was warmer than it actually was. By the time they fell asleep in the snow, it was too late.

Galahad arrived at the spot where Malcolm and Bors had been standing the previous watch. The two boys were leaning over the wall, their attention focused across the meadow.

'What's going on?' Galahad asked.

'Hope the kitchen nun got enough beauty sleep,' Malcolm said sarcastically. But Galahad thought the insult was half-hearted. 'Come and have a look at this.'

Galahad squinted into the distance, scanning the edge of the forest and the swaths of farmland and meadows that preceded it.

'What am I supposed to be looking at?'

'Between the aspens and the tall grass . . . Do you see them?' Bors said.

First, Galahad saw the flocks of birds – crows and larks attacking one another in the sky. And on the ground he saw the chaotic blur of fur. If he listened closely, he could almost hear their screeches, caws, and yowls in the distance.

'I've never seen anything like it,' said Malcolm, and Galahad thought, beneath Malcom's bluster, he detected a quiver of fear in his voice.

'They used to say the woods would give signs when danger was near,' Bors mused. 'At least, that's how the stories tell it. If that's not a sign, I don't know what is.'

'But what are they fighting about, I wonder?'

said Galahad. He scanned the landscape for more clues. 'Should we tell the queen?'

'Doubt there's much she could do with that information,' Malcolm said. 'Half the knights think she's unfit to rule, anyway. I don't see how a bunch of animals squabbling will help her argument.'

But Galahad was no longer looking at the animals fighting tooth and nail. The sun had slowly dawned behind them, rising up from the ocean like an egg yolk. The new light travelled down the road leading towards Camelot, illuminating a man slumped forward on a brown horse.

The haggard animal foamed at the mouth and limped from an arrow buried in its haunch. Dried blood covered the man's face like a red mask. He slipped from his horse and collapsed in a heap right outside the old cobbler's hut.

'Wake the queen!' Galahad shouted.

Chapter Thirty-Seven

Saxon weasels streamed into the grove with their weapons drawn. Their sudden appearance brought the existing battle to a standstill. Both the Darklings and Camelot knights stood frozen, unsure whose side the Saxons were on.

It wasn't until Saxon archers loosed their first volley of arrows into the crowd that both sides realised the new arrivals meant to attack them all.

Commander Kensington was the first to react.

'Camelot, fall back! To the castle!' the mouse shouted as she thrust her sword into the heart of an incoming stoat. If Commander Kensington felt panic or fear, no one would have known it. 'Larks, cover us!'

From above, General Flit whistled an urgent call to his soldiers.

Sir Owen picked up his horn and blew an off-kilter tune – the signal to retreat. Sir Alric tied a white banner to his helmet and started running for the castle. Other Camelot forces followed, sprinting as fast as they could across the meadow and towards the town.

The battalion of fighter larks dived into the grass, picking off the Saxon archers. Calib caught sight of Macie Cornwall scampering up the trunk of a tree, loosing arrow after arrow at the Saxons as she climbed.

Two weasels set upon Leftie. The lynx bled freely from a torn ear on his right side. He growled and hissed as he tried to keep both of the beasts within his line of vision. He twirled a scimitar in each paw, duelling both of his attackers at once.

Just as Leftie dispatched one weasel with a fierce elbow to the throat, the second one came sneaking from his right side – his blind spot.

'Leftie, to your right!' Calib shouted.

The big cat turned just in time to dodge an axe blow. As the weasel tried to recover, Leftie slammed the pommel of his scimitar onto the back of his skull. The creature crumpled into a heap. Leftie looked up at Calib, doubt showing in his yellow eye.

Blocked on one side by the Camelot forces and on the other by the advancing horde, the Darklings were hemmed into the grove. Leftie had a decision to make: continue to try to fight Camelot or turn to face the new foes.

'Crows, help the Camelot larks!' Leftie roared. The crows who had been furiously pecking at Sir Alric's mesh archer shields turned and began to dive-bomb along with the Camelot larks, desperately buying time for the grounded Camelot and Darkling animals to retreat.

Calib scanned the sky for Valentina but saw only strangers. To his horror, many of the birds were being felled before they could even reach the grass. He turned and ran after the other animals.

Suddenly, a weasel with a scar on his muzzle appeared in Calib's path. The creature had a row of sharp blades attached to each front paw, and his helmet was crowned with a ramming spear. The scarred weasel bared all his fangs at Calib as he charged towards him.

Without a sword, Calib was defenceless. He

scoured the ground for anything he could use as a weapon. There were a few abandoned weapons in the distance, but nothing within reach – nothing but the stringy withered roots of the aspen trees at his footpaws.

He braced his legs and faced the charging weasel, willing his heart to keep steady. At the last moment, when the weasel's spear tip was within piercing range, Calib shimmied to the side. He hooked his footpaw under a root and yanked. The stoat tripped over the lifted root and went sprawling onto his stomach.

Calib made to turn and run, but something jerked him back painfully. The weasel had grabbed his tail on the way down. Getting back on his paws, the weasel raised a blade to slash him.

Calib closed his eyes, certain that he would be killed that very instant. But then the weasel made a strange gargling sound. His black eyes rolled to the back of his head. He fell forward onto Calib. A spear was buried deep into the weasel's back.

Calib tried to wiggle out from underneath the dead weasel, but the creature was too heavy. A pair of paws appeared and rolled the corpse off Calib.

Sir Owen's grief-stricken face hovered over the dazed mouse.

'I was a fool, Calib. I thought . . . well . . .' Sir

Owen said, his voice trembling. He gestured to the fighting going on all around them. 'This is a fine mess, isn't it?'

Bleakly, they surveyed the scene. The enemy was relentless; even now, more and more weasels poured out from hiding. The Darkling and Camelot forces stood no chance.

They would all be slaughtered here. They would never make it back to the castle.

Calib saw Commander Kensington continue to fight as she tried to clear the way for the others to cross the field. Dead enemies lay around her. But he could see that she was becoming winded.

Sir Owen patted Calib on the back. 'Sir Trenton would be proud of you,' he said, his voice catching. The knight's eyes looked sad but resolute. 'I'll be sure to tell him that when I see him.'

Confused, Calib started to ask what he meant.

But Sir Owen was already charging towards the fray.

'For Camelot!' he shouted, his voice echoing up towards the trees.

'Wait!' Calib called out. 'You're going the wrong way!'

Sir Owen Onewhisker either didn't hear or didn't heed.

Calib started to dash after the knight. A new shadow passed over him, and his stomach dropped. More whizzed by, darkening the whole field. It was only when he noticed the shadows' extraordinarily large wingspan that he realised who they were.

'The owls,' he whispered in awe.

He recognised General Gaius leading the way. The rest of his parliament followed in a V formation. Their armour and helmets glittered against the newly risen sun.

The owls swooped down and began releasing large rocks from their clutches. They were loose stones from St Gertrude. With great accuracy, they dropped them on the Saxons. Commander Kensington looked up in astonishment as giant rocks crushed her closest foes.

General Gaius landed next to Calib and Kensington. His ear tufts were impeccably groomed. 'We'll cover you,' the general said to the commander. 'You must get every creature back within the castle walls.'

She did not need to be told twice.

'Retreat to the castle!' Commander Kensington called to the last of the warriors around her.

The owls, crows, and larks scooped up those who were injured. General Gaius picked up Calib by the shoulders and began to fly for the castle. The general dodged a number of arrows as he launched into the morning sky.

'General!' Calib cried. 'What convinced you to come?'

'When my scouts told me of the attack, I had half a mind to leave you groundlings to sort it out,' General Gaius said shortly. 'But then Seer Thaddeus kindly reminded me that I had failed to properly help you avoid this war. To make up for it, the owls will see this battle through with you.'

Calib looked below at the fleeing creatures. They had now reached the town. But the Saxon horde was in hot pursuit. Only so many creatures would make it behind the castle wall before they were overtaken.

As the animals ran through the cobblestone streets of Camelot, the Two-Leggers beginning their morning chores jumped back in alarm. Calib watched as some of the farmers and milkmaids shooed at the barrage of snarling weasels with brooms and shovels. This gave the Camelot and Darkling creatures precious seconds to outrace the Saxons.

Gaius and Calib landed in the castle courtyard. Around them, other birds swooped down, carrying the wounded. Foot soldiers from the Darklings and Camelot sides streamed through the doorways. Mice sentries ran about in a panic, shouting confused orders, no longer sure who the enemy was.

Finally, the last of the owls flew in, followed closely by Kensington and Leftie, who had been protecting the stragglers. The lynx, so fearless on the battlefield, needed three owls to lift him to his feet. His fur was dark and sticky with blood.

Devrin ran immediately to meet Commander Kensington. 'Commander! The Darklings . . . Do we turn them away?' she asked anxiously.

Though blood streamed down his face, Leftie gripped his scimitars tighter, ready to respond to whatever answer Commander Kensington gave. Calib held his breath and prayed for the right one.

Camelot's leader looked at a black squirrel who was sprinting towards the closing gate with an injured mouse on her back. And Macie, still in the distance, riding a Darkling crow and shooting arrows at the Saxons.

'No,' Kensington said. 'Let them all in.'

Chapter Thirty-Eight

The Goldenwood Hall echoed with the cries and whimpers of injured fighters.

They lay head to tail in the stands. Nurses and medics rushed about with stretchers, doing their best to tend to the wounded. Two shrews were treating Sir Alric from an arrow gash to the knee. A crow had a broken wing that was being set in a sling by his fellow crows. Those who were uninjured stood restlessly in their own groups on the arena floor. The Darkling and Camelot fighters eyed one another with suspicion.

The bell tower larks had taken most of the arrow

fire during the retreat. Very gently, Calib finished daubing the graze wound on a shuddering lark with a cooling cream made from crushed juniper berries.

'I'll need more gauze,' he called out, eyeing the rows of injured still waiting for care.

'We're all running low,' Devrin said. She was carefully setting a dislocated tail with the aid of Madame von Mandrake. 'The Two-Legger infirmary will have more supplies.'

'I can help Calib bring more supplies back,' said a familiar voice.

Calib whirled around.

Cecily stood there, smiling sheepishly, a lopsided bandage over her right ear. Her eyes were as clear and bright as ever.

'Cecily!' he exclaimed. Relief washed over him like a wave. Calib wrapped her in a tight hug. 'Thank Merlin, you're alive!'

'Ow, too hard!' Cecily gasped.

'Sorry.' Calib let go, suddenly self-conscious.

Cecily shrugged but was grinning nonetheless. 'It was nothing some healing herbs couldn't fix.'

'But Ginny said . . .'

'And when have you known Ginny *not* to exaggerate?' Cecily said. 'Now, come on, we need to hurry with the gauze.' She turned quickly, and Calib ran to keep up. Breathlessly, Calib briefed Cecily on all that had occurred since they separated, including the revelation that Sir Percival had planted the tooth all along.

'But what about you? What happened?' Calib asked.

'All I know is, I woke up in bed, and *Maman* was above me, screaming her head off,' Cecily said. 'It seems that everyone thought General Gaius had attacked me, so they chased him away before he had a chance to explain anything.'

They entered the Two-Legger infirmary by running along the curtain frames that divided patients' beds from one another. As Calib and Cecily passed one of the occupied beds, a small commotion was happening below. The word 'Saxon' drifted out to them, and Calib paused. He motioned for Cecily to stop as they peered over the bed.

Queen Guinevere, Sir Kay, and a number of older knights had gathered at the bedside of an unfamiliar man. The man was heavily bandaged, but he looked alert. He sat upright in an infirmary bed.

'Start from the beginning,' Queen Guinevere said.

'We first noticed it in the animals,' the man said,

his voice stony. 'For weeks, the woods had become overrun with weasels. Swarms of them. We couldn't make any sense of it. They attacked our crops and herds. The messenger birds were murdered in their cages.'

The man looked up, tears brimming in his eyes.

'And then one morning, the men came. They emerged from the swamp fog, silent like the wraiths from the days of old. They were armoured and without mercy.'

The messenger trembled. 'By the time I got away, the village was burning. I rode as fast as I could, but I fear it is too late. I told myself that I was running for help, but . . . in truth, I ran like a coward.'

'Lives may be saved yet because of your actions,' Guinevere said. 'Camelot has not seen war for many years. When these men attacked, did you get a good look at any of them? Did any of them say anything?'

The man squinted, trying to remember.

'They charged us with a banner – a white dragon against a red backing.'

Guinevere drew a sharp breath. The rest of the members of the Round Table exploded.

'Saxons attacking from inland! That can't be!' said Sir Kay. 'We defeated the Saxons years ago!'

'We should negotiate terms of surrender now,' said one anxious adviser, nervously chewing his nails, 'while there's still a chance they will let us live.'

Queen Guinevere stood up, her eyes blazing. 'Every able man with a mount must warn the other castles and ask for support.'

'Now, see here,' Sir Kay began, growing red in the face. 'Just because you married the king doesn't make you our ruler.'

'King Arthur united all of Britain so that we could stand together in a time of need.' Galahad, the page Calib remembered so well, spoke up, and the other knights gawked at him. Calib couldn't help being impressed. The Two-Legger was at least two heads shorter than everyone else in the room. 'The king is not here, but we must honour that belief.'

'We're sworn to follow whoever wields the Sword in the Stone. Where's *your* sword, little boy?' asked another knight.

Calib held his breath to hear what Galahad would say. But he only flushed red and mumbled something.

'And to think, Camelot once represented the bravest and finest knights in the land,' the queen said, her anger unmasked. 'How far we've all fallen.'

She looked around at the many knights who could not return her gaze.

On the curtain frame, Cecily shook her head.

'The Two-Leggers would rather stuff their ears full of cotton than listen to common sense,' she whispered to Calib.

'We have to tell Commander Kensington,' Calib whispered back. 'The Two-Legger Saxons will arrive soon! And half our number are injured, and the other half won't even look at one another, much less fight alongside one another!'

Cecily looked at Calib, and he couldn't quite tell what she was thinking.

'Not just Commander Kensington, but Leftie too,' she said. 'You're the only one who can convince both sides to listen, Calib. You have to convince them to face the Saxons as one army, or we'll be lost.'

Chapter Thirty-Nine

The tension inside Goldenwood Hall was as thick as honey from the comb but nowhere near as pleasant. From the corner of the room, Calib watched nervously as Commander Kensington limped onto the stage, shooing away a medic who came up to attend to her bite marks. Camelot's leader scanned the crowd.

'Where is General Flit?'

The larks in the hall looked at one another sadly.

'Felled by an arrow in the retreat.'

'And Sir Owen? Where is my second-in-command?' asked Commander Kensington.

Macie stepped forward, the fur under her eyes dark with dampness. 'Sir Owen . . . He covered for us – but he didn't make it.'

It felt as though someone had hooked Calib with a claw and gutted him. The first mouse ever to put a sword in Calib's paw, the mouse who had taught him the difference between a gauntlet and a tasset, his first teacher – gone.

Commander Kensington clenched her fist and pounded the table. She shook her head, her eyes clouded over with grief.

'May I speak?' The voice came from behind them.

It was Leftie.

The room hushed as the lynx slowly approached the stage. The lynx's eye patch was caked in blood, giving him a gruesome look. However, his weapons were sheathed. He held his paws up to show that they were empty.

The next seconds seemed to last an eternity, as if the very fate of Camelot were hanging on them. If the two animal groups could not agree, if they could not unite, then Calib knew that Thaddeus's vision would come true: Camelot would fall. Calib nervously flicked the tip of his tail back and forth and prayed that Leftie would be polite – and that

Commander Kensington would not lose her infamous temper.

'You are a fierce fighter, Kensington.' Leftie spoke first, his voice a rasp.

'As are you.' Commander Kensington nodded curtly. She paused before her next words. 'We believed you had murdered our leader, the late commander Yvers Christopher. But I see now that it was a deceit orchestrated by someone who had only Saxon interests at heart.'

Leftie nodded grimly. 'Your healer . . .'

'Sir Percival Vole did not show up to fight this morning,' Commander Kensington said, her voice growing angry. 'When I sent a page to check on him, she saw that his quarters have been emptied. The vole has fled.'

'Then we owe another apology,' Leftie said. 'Where is Calib Christopher, son of Sir Trenton Christopher, grandson of Commander Yvers Christopher?'

Calib's heart began to thump as one by one, each pair of eyes in the Goldenwood Hall turned towards him.

'Thank you, Calib,' Leftie said, 'for being brave enough to speak the truth when no one would listen.'

Calib saw Kensington's whiskers twitch – was the warrior mouse smiling? Just as quickly, the fleeting happiness was gone.

'I lost good beasts out there,' she said sombrely. 'But it's clear to me now that the Darklings were never at fault and neither were you, Calib. On behalf of Camelot, I apologise, and we offer you our thanks.'

Both leaders bowed to Calib. The young mouse felt heat rise in his cheeks, and his ears felt tingly. It wasn't the warmth of pride but of shame. If only he had been faster, stronger, and more sure of himself, maybe Sir Owen and the others would still be alive.

'But tell me, mousling,' Kensington said, eyeing him sharply. 'How is it that you managed to escape from your imprisonment?'

Calib gulped. He sensed instinctively that his mysterious encounter with Howell – with *Merlin* – must remain a secret. But he had no other explanation for his escape. Luckily, while he was still fumbling for excuses, Kensington raised a paw.

'On second thought,' she said with a strange twitching of her snout. 'Perhaps the less said, the better. Some mysteries are meant to remain just that.'

Calib exhaled, relieved. He then recounted what he had overheard on his way to the Two-Legger infirmary about the invading Saxon army. As he finished, General Gaius and two white snowy owls marched into the room. General Gaius gave a short salute with his wing and snapped his talons together. Merlin's Crystal sparkled against his chest.

'My lieutenants have all returned from their scouting missions. I'm afraid Calib's information is correct,' the owl began. 'Saxon Two-Leggers have arrived at the river, and the Saxon beasts are setting up siege weapons at the gate. By the looks of it, they are preparing to launch an assault on the castle before nightfall.'

Distraught, many animals began talking at once.

'We lost half the lark fleet to that ambush,' cried Sir Alric. 'We cannot hope to outlast a siege of both humans and beasts!'

'Our archers do not have enough arrows if the Saxon beasts begin to scale the walls,' Macie added grimly.

As the different bands of animals began to discuss and argue among themselves, Calib felt an idea try to take shape, but it was like a memory that slipped away from him whenever he tried to grasp it. He knew there was something to be done, something obvious he was missing . . .

'I don't see why we should risk our lives to defend a castle that we don't even live in,' sniffed a Darkling crow, nursing a broken wing. 'When all this is over, they'll kick us out without a word of thanks.'

'And yet you were more than eager to take shelter here with the rest of us,' Commander Kensington replied with a dirty look.

Calib's confidence began to unravel. Howell had said that all the creatures of Camelot must unite. Calib had brought them all here, but even with the castle creatures and Darklings united, how could they possibly stand up to the Saxon horde?

'Together in paw or tail, lest divided we fall and fail.' Calib read the words over the hall's entrance, the motto teasing him . . .

All the creatures of Camelot.

He recalled how the Two-Legger milkmaids had shooed away the Saxon weasels with their brooms and how some of the otters had provided cover for a few stranded Two Legger farmers to get to higher ground. He thought of Merlin's Promise, the vow that Commander Yvers had made to keep Camelot safe at all costs.

This was the path that Howell had guided him towards all along, from the moment they met in his cave. Surely, this protection also applied to the Two-Leggers who inhabited the castle as well.

And as for Merlin's Crystal . . . An ember of an idea sparked in Calib's mind.

'Master Thropper, could you boost me up?' Calib asked. The hare looked puzzled but obliged by lifting the mouse onto his shoulders.

Cupping his paws around his mouth, Calib called out over the hall, 'Listen!' The hubbub died down as thousands of eyes – dark and light, mouse and badger, lynx and crow – turned to look at him. He took a deep breath. 'Has anyone seen Lucinda the cat?'

Chapter Forty

Sir Edmund's quarters looked like they had been ransacked, with the drawers open and contents strewn across the floor. In fact, Galahad would have thought a thief had torn apart the room had Sir Edmund himself not been sitting in the middle of the mess, directing pages to pack his belongings.

'What's going on?' Galahad asked.

'We're getting out of here while we still have heads on our shoulders,' said the knight. He stood up, sniffing. 'You can join too. I'll need someone to prepare my meals.'

'You're *running away*?' Galahad asked, setting

the tray of dinner down with a clatter. 'But shouldn't you be defending the castle?'

'It's a lost cause, boy,' Sir Edmund said crankily, throwing a crumpled velvet duvet into a trunk. 'I don't fight for lost causes.'

'I don't believe you.' Galahad felt a flood of anger and shock grip him. 'And you call yourself a knight?'

'Watch your mouth, *kitchen boy*,' Sir Edmund said, colour mottling his cheeks.

'I'd rather do what good I can as a *kitchen boy* than stand idly by as a lord!' Galahad said angrily. He stormed out of the chambers, leaving a surprised Sir Edmund.

Galahad knew he had to see the queen. *Someone* had to do something about the oncoming attack. He was filled with an urgent desire to help, to fight. But Sir Edmund was right. What could he, a lowly kitchen boy, possibly do?

He found the queen pacing in the throne room. Her face looked strained. She was surrounded by her ladies-in-waiting. Malcolm, Bors, and many of the pages were also there. Galahad knew this meant that the knights they served had also fled.

'Apologies for intruding, Your Majesty, but it seems that Sir Edmund . . .' Galahad began.

'Yes, I know,' the queen said bitterly. 'Sir Edmund and many other knights like him.' She shook her head. She looked close to tears. 'It seems our only recourse is to surrender before we even put up a fight.'

The word 'surrender' hung in the room like a heavy blanket. Galahad shivered. He searched for something to say, some comfort he could give, some plan he could propose. But his mind was blank.

Then Galahad felt something brush against his shins. Guinevere's orange tabby had sauntered by – and, to Galahad's surprise, deposited a rolled piece of parchment right at his feet.

'Oh, Lucinda.' Guinevere picked up the ugly tabby. The queen was too preoccupied to see the piece of paper the cat had dropped. 'Always such a bother.'

The squashed face of the cat looked mildly offended.

Checking to make sure that no one was watching him, Galahad bent down and unrolled the piece of paper. His heart hiccupped.

On it, in the exact same cursive lettering as the message written in the sugar, was a short message: *Kom two Sward in Ston.*

Shocked, Galahad reread the message several

times. And then, all at once, it was as if a jigsaw puzzle in his brain had suddenly slotted into place, and he understood.

'Don't worry,' Galahad said. His voice echoed in the enormous chamber, and he looked up to find everyone staring at him. But he felt no fear. 'I think I have a plan.'

Chapter Forty-One

From far below, a glint caught Calib's eye. 'There!' he yelled into the wind.

General Gaius nodded once to show that he had heard him. Calib clung to the owl's feathers as they veered downwards. Looking below, the mouse was relieved to see that Lylas, the Darkling badger, was able to keep up with the owl.

'Do you think we'll get there in time?' General Gaius called to Calib. 'Are you *sure* this is the only way to get the Two-Leggers to join the fight?'

'I think so,' he said. 'The Two-Leggers believe that whoever pulls the Sword in the Stone is

Camelot's true leader. If we manage it, they'll have no choice but to rally behind the sword wielder. We need to show them how to fight again.'

'But will the Two-Legger understand your message?' he pressed.

Calib wanted to say, *Yes, of course.* But deep down he wasn't sure. The mice and Two-Leggers had never worked together before. At best, they had lived in a state of precarious truce. At worse, they had been all-out enemies, with the mice raiding the Two-Leggers' kitchen, and the Two-Leggers fighting back with brooms and traps and, occasionally, kitchen knives.

It was no wonder that the war council had been incredulous when Calib suggested that they ask the humans to join the animals in the castle's defence.

'If they want to run, let them run!' an old mouse-knight had snorted from her spindle chair. 'Good riddance to those cowards, I say! Back in my day, a knight was a knight!'

The council had remained doubtful even after Calib repeated what Sir Kay had said in the infirmary: that the human knights were sworn to follow the Sword in the Stone.

But even that announcement had drawn opposing murmurs from the creatures in the Goldenwood

Hall. It wasn't until Leftie spoke up that they began to consider Calib's plan in earnest.

'I, for one, trust you, Calib Christopher,' the big cat had announced to the room, laying down one of his sharp blades at Calib's feet, in front of the awed crowd. 'Last time we didn't heed your warning, we paid a very high price. I will not make that mistake a second time.'

In the end, Commander Kensington organised a small expedition, led by General Gaius, Sir Alric, and the Darkling badger Lylas Whitestripe. Calib and Cecily were to accompany them to the Sword in the Stone, using Howell's secret passageway to escape the castle without being detected.

By using the tunnel, the group had managed to avoid the attention of the Saxon weasels lying in wait at the edges of the castle's fields. Nonetheless, there was still a chance a Saxon might spot them as they made the final leg of their journey to the small vale that concealed the Sword in the Stone.

Looking down at the battle-scarred badger carrying Sir Alric and Cecily, Calib wondered what it meant that Leftie had insisted that the surly Lylas join them. Did the lynx even expect them to come back alive?

As Gaius swooped down into the clearing, Calib's

breath hitched in his chest. Somehow, the Sword in the Stone seemed even more majestic, even more *magical*, than it had when he'd seen it earlier. In the sun, the blade dazzled like a bolt of lightning.

Gaius alighted gently on the sword's hilt, and a moment later, Lylas, Sir Alric, and Cecily appeared. For a second, all the animals stood there in silence, bound up in the beauty of the strange sight.

Calib roused himself first. 'All right, we need to figure out a way to get the sword out of the stone.'

'If the Two Leggers have yet to manage this, what chance do you think we have?' asked Lylas.

'We have the key!' Calib pointed to Merlin's Crystal.

Everyone looked at Calib, confused.

'Merlin's Crystal is supposed to unlock a *great strength*, right?' The words tumbled from him in his excitement to explain. 'Well, what if the *great strength* meant is the Sword in the Stone!'

Lylas slammed his paw to his chest. 'It could be entirely possible, young mousling. None of us ever thought it could be a Two-Legger weapon.'

Calib nodded. 'Exactly. Gaius, could you bring the crystal closer to the sword?'

The owl dipped his head to dangle Merlin's treasure near the blade. After a few uncertain seconds, the crystal and the sword suddenly began to glow the same milky blue. The runes that decorated the blade seemed to shimmer and change shape.

'Old Magic,' Sir Alric said in an awed whisper. He wiped away a tear that rolled down his snout. 'I never thought I'd see the day . . .'

'Did it – Do you think it did something?' Cecily asked. 'I mean, do you think we can pull it out now?'

'Step aside,' Lylas rumbled, 'and I will prove to you that badger strength is unparalleled.'

But though the badger pulled and tugged at the hilt with all his might, the sword remained as stuck as it ever had. Lylas began to punch the rock.

'What are you doing?' Gaius asked.

'Trying . . . to . . . loosen . . . the . . . sword,' Lylas grunted between breaths. 'Stuck . . . solid.'

Calib's heart sank. His plan wasn't working. He had failed them all.

'We could try to chisel it out,' Sir Alric suggested. He had climbed up to the sword's hilt and had begun measuring it with a ruler made from leftover embroidery thread.

'We don't have time!' Cecily said, anxiously waving her sword. 'And the Saxons could find us any minute!'

'This doesn't make sense.' Calib sat down on his haunches, trying not to let defeat overcome him. They were so close to completing their mission! He was so sure Merlin's Crystal was the key. There *had* to be a way to remove the sword.

Sitting on the ground, Calib noticed for the first time that the crack in the stone widened at the bottom of the rock, creating a slight crevice at its base. Perhaps when Lylas punched the sword, it had widened the split. Calib's ears began to tingle. The large fissure looked just like the entrance to Howell's cave, only mouse-sized.

Calib sprinted towards it. Peering in, he saw that it extended back, creating a passageway into the stone just big enough for a mouse to squeeze through.

'Sir Alric, come quickly!' he said. 'Lylas and Cecily, stand guard with Gaius.'

The badger lifted the mouse-knight from where he stood on the stone and placed him next to Calib.

Gesturing for Sir Alric to follow him, Calib squeezed into the passageway. After only a few mouse lengths, the tunnel opened up into a small cavern within the stone.

In the centre of the cavern, the lethally sharp tip of the Two-Legger sword bathed the cavern in an eerie blue light. The sword had cut all the way through the granite, stopping just short of resting on the dirt floor. The runes on the blade glowed strongest at the tip.

'Sir Alric, are you able to read these runes?' Calib asked.

The knight squinted a moment. 'It's been a long while since I learned them, but I think it reads: "There is great power in small warriors." However, there's one mark here that doesn't make any sense.'

The knight pointed to the last one etched closest to the point of the sword. A tingle raced up Calib's spine. He ran his paw down the blade carefully, tracing the edges of the rune. It was larger than the rest – about as big as Calib's arm. And it was in the shape of a dagger.

'This isn't a rune at all!' Calib said. 'Quick, we need the crystal!'

Sir Alric was already running out of the crevice, and Calib followed only a whisker length behind.

After listening to the mice's careful explanation, Gaius bowed his head so that Calib and Cecily could pull the crystal over his tufts. The crystal was even more beautiful up close. It was as clear as a raindrop and seemed to hum with its own excited energy. Or maybe it was only reflecting the excitement that Calib felt in his own heart.

Using all their strength, the three mice were able to pull the unwieldy crystal into the cavern.

Once there, Sir Alric and Cecily helped Calib prop the crystal into place. With a satisfying click, Merlin's Crystal slid into the empty shape of the rune.

For a moment, nothing happened, but then the sword exploded with blinding light. Calib held his paws over his face to protect his eyes from the brilliant rays.

There was a loud cracking sound, and the sword dislodged from the stone ceiling. It slid down in a sudden avalanche of pebbles and dust and then thudded to the bottom of the cavern.

Sir Alric let out an undignified whoop of joy, and Cecily threw her arms around Calib's neck. Blushing, Calib disentangled himself and rushed over to examine the ruins.

Merlin's Crystal had melted into the sword, turning into a dagger-shaped rune. Calib put his paw to it, and it felt cool. There would be no removing the crystal from the blade now.

Sir Alric and Cecily were still cheering when Gaius's worried voice echoed towards them.

'We've got company!' he squawked.

'Who is it?' Cecily asked, planting her footpaws into the attack stance.

'Two-Leggers from Camelot!'

Calib slipped through the fissure and into the sun, turning to look where Gaius was staring.

A boy with oversize ears and a determined expression appeared, riding a stubborn-looking white pony, and Calib could hear that more Two-Leggers followed behind him.

'What do we do?' Lylas asked, straightening his breastplate.

Calib smiled.

'We welcome them.'

Chapter Forty-Two

As Galahad approached the Sword in the Stone, he was not surprised at all to see a small tawny mouse perched upon its hilt. He watched the mouse rise onto his hind legs and wave his paw, almost in a greeting.

A group of mice, an owl, and a badger wearing a tortoise shell on his front stood guard. The badger reared up and held out his fists like a boxer. The great horned owl spread its wings and screeched.

Galahad heard the crowd of loyal Camelot servants and squires murmur uneasily behind him. It had actually been more surprising to Galahad that all the squires had offered him their protection and support.

'It's better than watching the parade of cowards at the castle,' Malcolm had said, and Galahad knew then that his days of torment were over. 'I'll follow you, Galahad.'

Malcolm now stood behind him, a large poleaxe clutched in his hand while Bors drew his sword.

'I've never seen animals like this,' Bors whispered, wide-eyed.

'Maybe you haven't been looking,' Galahad said.

He dismounted his pony and carefully approached the tawny mouse, half-expecting him to scamper away. But the mouse stood completely still.

Galahad held out his hand tentatively, just like the first time they had met. The mouse seemed to consider this for a moment. Then he leaped onto the boy's hand and, with barely any pressure at all, scampered from the boy's wrist to his shoulder. Galahad could feel the soft tickle of the mouse's fur against his neck.

Galahad thought he understood what to do next.

He looked at the sword, admiring the masterfully forged blade that gleamed like fire. He wrapped his fingers around the hilt and pulled. A gasp went through the crowd.

Effortlessly, the sword that had budged for no one else glided out of the stone.

For a moment, Galahad felt weightless. A powerful current coursed through him, and his senses seemed to extend to all the woods around him. He closed his eyes and felt the weight of his body on the moss beneath his feet. He felt the wind tickling the branches of the trees overhead and the warmth of the sunlight on their leaves. He could feel the stomp of boots as the first of the Saxon army began to tread the charred ground of St Gertrude's ruins. All at once, Galahad was aware of the many voices the woods possessed. They came to him in a gentle chorus of pleas. He heard the babble of the river protesting the intruders who had sloshed through its shallows with their weapons and their beasts.

'Seek the Lady of the Lake,' a voice whispered in his ear. He thought it might be the voice of the wind. 'She will show you the way.'

Galahad opened his eyes and held the sword high over his head, its sharp point raised towards the sky. The flat of the blade reflected the sunlight with a golden flash. He hardly noticed that before him, people were falling one by one to their knees. They bowed to him and to the power of the sword, which had been destined to reveal the true leader of Camelot.

'We have to go back to the castle,' Galahad said, and his voice sounded louder and deeper than it ever had before. 'The Saxons have reached St Gertrude's. Today, we fight!'

Chapter Forty-Three

The whole group, both animal and Two-Legger, raced together back to the castle, with Calib seated on Galahad's shoulder.

The mouse calculated that if Galahad was right and the Saxon Two-Leggers had passed St Gertrude, they had only a half an hour before the human army joined the weasels at the edge of the Darkling Woods.

They had to get back in time!

As Galahad thundered across the drawbridge, the sword remained sheathed.

'I have the Sword in the Stone!' the boy shouted, cupping his hand around his mouth and waving his other arm.

It took a second for the castle inhabitants to stop their travel preparations and realise what the boy had said. But as Galahad rode forward into the courtyard, the clamour died around him.

Calib slipped a little as Galahad stopped his pony in the centre of the courtyard. The mouse looked from the boy's shoulder onto a sea of faces – some of them suspicious, some of them hopeful, most of them flat-out disbelieving.

There was a commotion behind him, and Calib turned to see Sir Kay and the rest of the knights come out from the stables, their horses saddled. Calib thought they must have been about to mount their chargers and ride away from Camelot.

'*You?* You're telling me that *you* pulled the Sword in the Stone?' said Sir Kay. 'Even Arthur's feat, as great as his skill was, was a stretch of the imagination, but *you*?!'

Sir Edmund strode up to Galahad, glaring openly in his face. 'Most likely this boy found a sword in a scrap heap and now thinks he can play us all for fools.'

'Only a true knight could pull the Sword from the Stone.' Sir Kay narrowed his eyes. 'The honour is not meant for a poor kitchen boy.'

Calib scowled. What did they know about what a kitchen boy – or mouse, for that matter – could do?

'Then maybe it's not a knight that we need,' said Galahad. The boy unsheathed the sword from his scabbard and held it aloft.

Calib shivered. A current passed through the crowd, as if an invisible, magical wind had lifted the hairs on everyone's necks. Sir Kay, Sir Edmund, and the rest of the knights with their bulging travel packs went silent, their eyes wide as goose eggs. It was more than a sword. Lit up by the sun, dazzling with ancient runes, it seemed like a promise.

For a second, Calib thought he heard Howell's voice, but it came to him so softly he could not make out its message. Then the wind whipped that away.

'Growing up, the stories were all the same.' Galahad spoke clearly, and Calib thought he did not at all look the part of the raggedy kitchen boy. He looked like a true knight. 'The hero always comes to the rescue. But we cannot wait for others to save us. This day, we must be our own heroes.

We are the last defenders of Camelot! Now, who will stand with me?'

Malcolm raised his sword first. 'All of Camelot is sworn to follow the Sword in the Stone! If a kitchen boy can pull the Sword in the Stone, then we can defend the castle without King Arthur!'

Calib watched with satisfaction as one by one, the Two-Leggers of Camelot drew their swords, crying out their loyalty to the castle and to Britain. They raised their weapons – some of them no more than brooms and pitchforks – in answer to Galahad's plea. They shouted and stamped and filled the courtyard with rumbling noise.

Galahad's ears flushed with heat – his plan was working!

Suddenly, a frantic cacophony erupted from the bell tower. This was not the orderly chiming familiar to all the inhabitants of Camelot. This was a clanging crash that sounded like every bell in the tower was being rung at once, as hard as possible.

It was an alarm.

Somewhere on the walls a Two-Legger was shouting.

'Invaders at the gates! Thirtyscore and counting!' There was a rusty creak as the drawbridge was slowly raised.

'Time to go, Valentina!' Calib whistled for the crow. She dived neatly and scooped Calib up from Galahad's shoulder. Calib regretted not saying good-bye, but Galahad was too busy giving orders to the Two-Leggers. Besides, if they managed to defend Camelot from the invaders, there would be plenty of time to talk later.

From his vantage point on Valentina's back, Calib could see flashing metal, marching from the edge of the Darkling Woods and the telltale bend of the grass that told him that the weasels had returned.

Valentina flapped to the ramparts, where the animal army was waiting.

'You're back!' Commander Kensington shouted as Valentina landed. For a moment, the stern commander looked as happy as a small mousling with a fresh piece of cheese. 'Thank Merlin! Did it work?'

'I think so,' Calib said, slipping off Valentina's feathers. 'We managed to free the Sword in the Stone. The Two-Leggers are sworn to follow whoever holds it.'

'Let's just hope it's not too late,' Kensington said grimly. She looked at Calib as his fellow pages – Cecily, Devrin, Warren, and Barnaby – gathered around him.

'Stick together,' Kensington said. 'Those are my only orders to you. Make Sir Owen proud. Make Commander Yvers proud. Make Camelot proud.'

Then the commander of Camelot put on her helmet and walked to the front of the walls. 'On your guard!' she bellowed.

Crows, owls, and larks took to the air in an explosion of feathers. Badgers and otters hefted axes and spears as they headed towards the gates. Hares wielding staves and slings bounded away towards the corner towers. And all along the walls, mice and squirrels poured out of Camelot's secret passages to take up positions along the battlements as they waited for the enemy to attack.

Calib's heartbeat was as loud as a beating drum. A thousand things could go wrong in battle, and so much was on the line. He began to nibble on his whiskers.

'Good luck, Calib,' Cecily said, sidling up next to him. She squeezed his paw. 'And thank you. Without you, we wouldn't even have a fighting chance.'

Calib's ears burned. He looked at Cecily. He wanted to tell her something brave, to ask her to be careful in the fight ahead, but there was nothing he could think of that didn't sound foolish in his head.

Instead, he simply drew his sword and gave a nod to his friends – the pages of Camelot. Cecily raised her own sword, as did Devrin, and even Barnaby, who for once, held his sword steady.

'Watch out!' Macie yelled from somewhere along the wall. A massive wooden shaft sliced through the air above Calib's head, embedding itself into the side of the wall. It was easily as long as ten mice laid nose to tail.

The Saxons had begun their attack.

'Right,' Lylas barked as he appeared beside the pages. 'You little mice, follow me!'

The badger took off at a run. Calib followed, trying to keep pace with Devrin as she darted ahead. Barnaby and Cecily followed close behind.

They passed a pair of Two-Legger soldiers running in the opposite direction. The soldiers spared a confused glance for the sight of five mice chasing after a badger wearing a tortoise shell, but only a glance. They had more urgent concerns.

'For Camelot! Knights of the Round Table, to me!'

Even through the chaotic din of the battle, Calib's ears pricked up at the sound of Galahad's voice. He saw the boy in the courtyard below, sitting astride his pony, waving the sword above his head.

Knights and soldiers and townsfolk all gathered around him, pressing towards the castle gates. Mostly unnoticed, a small army of hares and otters and mice followed closely at their heels.

As Calib and the pages reached the western wall, more arrows followed, both enormous Two-Legger ones and smaller animal ones. Calib slung acorns down at the enemy, even as he narrowly missed the arrows that were sailing over the high castle walls. Each arrow that made it over the battlements hit the ground with a deafening thud so loud that Calib almost didn't hear Devrin's cry of alarm.

'Enemy scaling the western wall! They have ladders!'

Calib looked just as a tall weasel with greasy fur vaulted over and hissed savagely at the pages.

He had a vicious-looking knife between his teeth, and an axe strapped to his back, the hilt protruding above one shoulder. He grinned around the knife, flashing yellow fangs. He spread his arms wide in a dramatic bow.

'Greetings, mousling,' the weasel said, spitting the knife into his paw. 'I shall try to make your death as quick as possible.'

Chapter Forty-Four

There was no time even to feel fear.

Calib turned to face the weasel head-on. Drawing on all the strength he had, he held aloft his sword and pointed it at the weasel's chest. He shouted the bravest thing that came to his head:

'Turn back in the name of Calib, son of Sir Trenton Christopher, and the memory of my grandfather, Yvers the Great!'

The weasel hesitated for only half a second, and Calib thought, to his surprise, that the weasel was afraid. But then the Saxon began to chuckle, a cruel little snicker that grew loud and full of hate.

'I adore a tasty Christopher mouse! I will tear your chest open just like I did your granpappy's!'

Calib felt his body go rigid. Now, clearer than ever, he saw the long, lean shadow that leaped onto the stage, and the giant bladed paws.

A weasel. A weasel assassin.

Calib was standing in front of Yvers's true killer. The need for vengeance erupted inside his heart. Before Calib could help himself, he was screaming in rage.

'FOR CAMELOT!'

Calib threw himself at the weasel with all his strength. He brandished the sword over his head and brought it slamming down – but the weasel swerved to the side and nimbly parried the blow. As Calib passed him, the weasel delivered a swift kick to Calib's back.

Calib fell on his stomach, winded. Coughing and gasping, he flipped around to get up. But before he could stand, the weasel stepped on his chest. He positioned his blade-laced paw at Calib's throat.

'Say hello to your grandfather for me,' he sneered.

'Now, hold on just a moment.'

Never had Calib been more relieved to hear

Warren's mocking voice. 'You never introduced yourself,' Warren said, leaning against his sword casually, as if he had not a care in the world. 'You didn't give us a chance to welcome you to Camelot.'

The weasel rounded on him. 'The name is Ragnar,' he spat out. 'And I don't want your welcome. I do not go where I am welcome. I go where it pleases me to go, and do as it pleases me to do.'

Warren sighed dramatically and shook his head. 'That might be good enough in . . . wherever you lot are from. But here in Camelot we believe in honour and chivalry. And I have to say, the way you're going about this attack isn't very chivalrous.'

The weasel laughed scornfully. 'Chivalry? Honour? There is no honour in war, foolish mouse. There is only fighting and killing, winning and losing. A lesson you will not live long enough to learn.'

'Fighting and winning,' said Barnaby. Calib squeaked with surprise – Barnaby had managed to sneak up behind the weasel. He slashed at the beast's hindquarters, scoring a deep cut across his flank. 'I think we get that part.'

Ragnar yowled in pain and turned to face

Barnaby. Barnaby drew back. Calib saw that he was trembling, but he managed to parry the weasel's fresh attack – eyes open for once. Calib took the opportunity to dart in and land a blow on the beast's exposed shoulder, ducking under a furious swipe as the weasel tried to keep all three of his opponents in his line of sight. As he made another lunge at Warren, Cecily and Barnaby leaped onto his neck, biting and pummelling him about the shoulders just below his battered helmet.

With a violent twist, Ragnar managed to stop Cecily from clinging to his back. And a sweep of his tail caught Barnaby in the midsection, tossing him against the parapet. Breathing heavily now, Ragnar seemed to have lost most of his swagger. Now, there was only cold rage in the sneer he turned on Calib and Warren.

'Lesson is over. Now, you die.'

Ragnar slid the knife into his belt, and in one smooth motion drew the axe from behind his back. The shaft was bright metal, but the blade itself was covered in some dark liquid. Poison.

With a vicious hiss, Ragnar charged, swinging the axe. Calib and Warren stumbled back, trying to keep out of range of the blade. There was no chance of landing counterblows now. Ragnar had twice the reach of their swords.

Calib took another step backwards and felt cold stone on his tail. Ragnar had them cornered.

Calib held his sword in front of him, ready for one last desperate stand. Beside him, Warren did the same. The poisoned axe gleamed dully in the red afternoon sun.

Then a sudden movement behind Ragnar's left ear caught Calib's eye. Devrin was waving frantically to Calib from across the parapet.

No, not waving. She had her sling out, spinning above her head. But good as Devrin was with her sling, Ragnar was wearing thick armour, and a helmet. From where she was standing, there was no part of him that she could hit. Unless . . . Calib's eyes widened as he understood what she intended for him to do.

He would have only one chance. He knew that. He took a deep breath and remembered what Devrin had always repeated: he just needed to relax. He needed to believe. He needed to lean into it.

'Say good-bye to this world, mousies,' Ragnar hissed as he raised the axe and prepared to sweep it down on them.

With a snap of her wrist, Devrin's sling went slack. Calib had only a brief glimpse of something hurtling towards the weasel, shooting past his head, close enough to graze his ear. Calib swung his sword with all of his might.

The impact of the stone against the flat of the sword sent shockwaves through Calib's paws. As fast as Devrin had launched it at Calib, the ricochet was just as fast. The batted stone smashed into Ragnar's face, catching him right between the eyes. The force of the blow knocked him backwards. The weasel dropped his axe and took several unsteady steps, his eyes unfocused. He stumbled to the edge of the wall and teetered there for a moment. Then Ragnar fell, toppling off the rampart into a prickly bush far below.

Calib exhaled a long shuddering breath. Warren stared at the unconscious weasel in amazement. 'Wow. I can't believe I ever made fun of your Hurler technique. That was incredible.'

'Thanks,' Calib said. He felt suddenly uncomfortable. They hated each other . . . didn't they? 'And, um, thank you. You know, for having my back.'

'It was the least I could do,' Warren said with a shrug. But just as quickly, his casualness disintegrated and his shoulders slumped. 'Listen, Calib. This is all my fault. If I had been brave earlier and told Kensington the truth . . . I honestly didn't know Sir Percival was lying. I just want to be a knight so badly.'

'Believe me,' Calib said with a heavy sigh. 'I understand more than you know.'

There was a tremendous splintering sound from the main gate.

Calib watched as the knights of Camelot, led by Galahad, rushed to defend it, but already Saxon Two-Leggers were crossing the moat and streaming through the broken drawbridge doors and into the courtyard.

Looking at the rampart above the gate, Calib could make out a tall figure in a flowing gown that could only be Queen Guinevere, attended by the other ladies of the court. At the queen's signal, the ladies lifted several large kettles and emptied their contents of boiling oil onto the heads of the invaders. Screams and shouts erupted as the scalded Saxons writhed in pain, but still more and more kept coming in.

The queen then plucked a crossbow off a fallen Saxon. The man had just made it over the wall before two owls dropped an icy rock on his head.

Setting one of his arrows to the crossbow, Guinevere began to pick off targets from above the gate. Meanwhile, the larks provided cover for the ladies-in-waiting as they retreated farther into the castle.

All around him, Calib could see animals and humans working together against the enemy. The otters were skating across the frozen moat in pairs, tripping Saxon foot soldiers crossing the drawbridge with a piece of rope drawn taut between them. Beyond the moat, he could see Saxon horses stumbling on the holes dug by the garden moles.

Despite all these triumphs, more and more Saxons still gained ground. Calib knew that they would not be able to hold off so many assailants for very much longer.

Then came a strange tremor that shook the walls all the way to the ramparts. It was a rhythmic thumping that rose up from the ground, as if something very heavy and large was bounding closer at a fast gait.

'Do you feel that?' Calib asked Cecily.

Cecily's tail twitched, and she pressed her ear to the ground. Suddenly, she began to laugh.

'It looks like someone *did* decide to come after

all!' And she pointed towards an enormous dark blur rushing for the castle.

With a gigantic roar, Berwin the Bear charged through the broken gate and into battle.

Chapter Forty-Five

Berwin the Beastly swept through the unsuspecting Two-Legger Saxons like a scythe. His rusty armour protected his back from the onslaught of arrows. They bounced off Berwin like raindrops.

Growling ferociously, he trampled and slashed at the frightened Saxons around him with wild abandon. His eyes were wide with rage, his jaws snapping.

'Go, Berwin!' Calib and Cecily shouted as the bear, using only a single paw, began pushing an entire squadron of invaders back through the broken doors and into the moat.

Valentina landed on the wall, blocking Calib's view of Berwin. On her feet she wore a pair of spurs with lethally sharpened prongs. 'We need more warriors at the eastern ramparts!' she cawed. 'The Saxons are climbing in from every direction!'

Cecily and Calib found Commander Kensington, fighting off five Saxon creatures at once. Every motion she made was fluid and balanced, each attack gliding smoothly into a defensive stance, which in turn flowed back into a counterattack. In a matter of moments, she had dispatched two stoats, two weasels, and a pine marten.

Spying Calib and Cecily, Kensington beckoned them to her side. 'You two, cover me.' She pointed towards the western wall. 'I'm making my way to *him*.'

Perched atop the stone battlements, surrounded by Saxon archers, a familiar round face was watching the action unfold below him. He smiled when he saw the mice, revealing a mouth full of rotten teeth.

'Is that . . . ?' Cecily started to ask.

'Sir Percival Vole!' Calib almost choked. It was one thing to suspect a knight of treason, but it was quite another to see him standing in league with the enemies who were trying to kill them. Anger vibrated through every bone in Calib's body, right down to his tail. His grandfather had trusted Percival, and the vole repaid that trust with deceit and lies.

Calib needed no more motivation. He and Cecily and Kensington hacked and blocked their way across the wall, always with one eye on Sir Percival. They had almost reached him when the vole turned to the archers beside him and pointed in their direction.

'Cover!' yelled Commander Kensington, and the three of them dived behind a broken breastplate that might have once fit an otter.

But before the archers could fire, a scraggly yellow lynx leaped up into view. Leftie barrelled into the archers, knocking them aside like ragdolls. Then with a single swipe of his clawed paw, he sent Sir Percival flying off the wall to land at Kensington's feet.

Calib, Cecily, and Kensington stood over the fat vole, swords pointed at his chest. Percival looked dazed. He was bleeding from a long gash across his left cheek, and he appeared to have lost several of his rotted teeth. But as he regained his senses, his look of confusion was replaced by one of fear.

'Ah, K-Kensington!' he stammered. 'Thank goodness you've rescued me from these vile Saxons! They were about to—'

'Spare us, Percival.' Kensington's voice was flat and humourless. 'We know what you've done. There's no time to give you the slow punishment your crimes deserve, so a quick death will have to do.'

She raised her sword as Percival cowered in terror. But before she could strike, a booming voice sounded across the wall, a voice so sharp and powerful that creatures on both sides paused in midcombat to listen.

'Stay your paw, Commander. That one is under my protection.' A red-hooded figure sat astride a hawk. A gold Grecian mask hid the face of the creature beneath. Snakeskin gloves covered its lean paws.

'And who, might I ask, do I have the *dis*pleasure of speaking to?' Commander Kensington asked.

'I am known as the Manderlean,' the masked creature said.

Calib's focus sharpened. So this was the Manderlean. The air seemed to shimmer around the creature. 'I am here to offer terms for your surrender. You cannot hope to defeat us with your paltry numbers.'

Leftie spat at the ground.

'Then you should know we would rather die than surrender to the likes of you.'

'Wish granted,' the Manderlean hissed, spurring the winged steed forward. The hawk reared up and tried to take out Leftie's remaining eye with its cruelly hooked beak. Commander Kensington parried with her sword, sustaining a gash to her own face instead.

It was as if the world in front of Calib slowed down, and he saw Sir Percival seize his opportunity to escape. Scooting from underneath everyone's drawn swords, the vole ran to the hawk and leaped behind the Manderlean.

Calib bolted after Percival, latching onto the hawk's tail. The bird dipped down from the weight.

The Manderlean spun around and looked straight into Calib's eyes with two black holes. The masked creature gave a short bark of cruel laughter and kicked Calib in the snout. Losing his grip, Calib fell back onto the rampart with a bone-jarring thud.

Another wave of vermin surged over the wall in their wake.

Everything was a mess of fur and blood and metal. Calib stood up, trying to quell his panic. Even with a hundred swords pulled from a hundred stones, even with a bear who had found his courage, they could not hope to turn back the tide of invaders. Camelot was doomed.

Calib felt a final resolve harden his spine. He drew in his breath for a battle cry. If this was to be their fate, let it be one for the legends.

Chapter Forty-Six

A chorus of horns suddenly sang out from the east, and a cry of dismay caught in Calib's throat. Could there be even *more* Saxons joining the fray?

But he saw at once that this was not the case. The Saxons hesitated. They looked at one another, obviously confused.

So who had sounded the horns?

A great winged shadow passed over Calib's head and circled back to alight in front of him.

'Hop on, Calib Christopher,' General Gaius said. 'You deserve to see this.'

Calib scrambled onto the general's back,

holding tight to the feathers at his neck, and the two took off. As they passed over the gates and above the fields beyond, Calib saw a long row of Two-Legger knights on horseback riding over the crest of the hill. The setting sun illuminated their banners and armoured steeds. They formed the shape of a V and raised their weapons – their spears, axes, and swords aimed directly at the Saxon forces.

'Can you make out their banners?' Calib squinted at the two knights who stood at the tip of the formation. Their sigils were too far away for him to see.

'The leader bears three crowns against a blue backing, his lieutenant bears a white banner with three red stripes,' General Gaius reported.

'It's King Arthur and Sir Lancelot!' Calib said excitedly. 'The knights have come home!'

The horns sounded a second time. This time they were joined by a powerful rallying cry from the knights defending the castle.

King Arthur and his fearsome knights rushed down the hill towards the stunned Saxons. Their horses pounded the ground with their hooves, kicking up mounds of dirt. Their spears glinted red in the sun.

General Gaius turned a graceful circle in the air, and Calib saw that inside the castle, the badgers already had most of the Saxon weasels running while a large, stocky page led a surprise attack on the northern tower. A new energy surged through the defenders with the arrival of the human knights, and the battle turned quickly.

Fighting on two fronts, the Saxon army lost what ground they had gained. Many of them found themselves trapped between the advancing armies.

King Arthur had brought at least a hundred more knights with him, the finest and strongest in the land. Each knight was worth ten of the Saxons. There was Sir Yvain, who once tamed a lion, and Sir Bedivere, who had once defeated a giant.

Slowly at first, and then quick as the retreating tide, the Saxon forces began to fall back. Calib let out a ragged cheer as General Gaius continued to sweep over the battlefield, giving Calib full view of Camelot's victory. A grin broke out across Calib's face, one that was so big that he wondered if his whiskers had fallen off to make room for it.

Suddenly there was a cry from General Gaius, and Calib grabbed wildly at the owl's tawny feathers as it banked hard. He looked down at the battlefield to see what had made the bird shriek.

His heart stopped.

Arrows had lodged in Berwin's armour like porcupine quills. The bear's mouth was foaming. He bled from many gashes across his arms and legs, but his eyes were focused as he galloped straight on.

Calib swivelled his head to see what had so gripped the bear and saw that a last group of Saxons were preparing a trebuchet against the castle. One that would release a boulder big enough to take out the corner tower where Queen Guinevere was reattaching Camelot's flag to a rampart.

Just as the Two-Leggers prepared to slice the rope and let the boulder fly, Berwin lunged.

The entire structure crashed to the ground, crushing the Saxons underneath. The bear stood on his hind legs and gave a victorious roar.

But from Gaius's back, Calib could see what Berwin could not. One of the Saxons was not yet dead.

'Watch out!' the mouse yelled, but he was too high up to be heard.

As Berwin towered over the Saxon, the Two-Legger

pulled himself up into a crouch and drove his sword up under the bear's breastplate, burying it to the hilt.

Calib's scream was lost somewhere between his heart and his throat as Berwin looked down, his face changing from surprise to great pain.

'Go! Go!' Calib yelled, urging Gaius towards the bear.

Berwin dropped down on all fours and tried to limp to the shelter of the Darkling trees. The wounded Saxon crawled away, but Berwin ignored him. With every step he took, a terrible grimace flashed across the bear's face.

As Gaius dove down to the bear, Berwin collapsed, massive paws sprawling in the snowy dirt.

Calib vaulted off General Gaius. 'Get a healer!' he yelled to the owl before he even hit the ground. Gaius nodded and flew to the castle while Calib raced to the bear's side.

'Berwin,' the mouse said, skidding to a stop before the great beast. 'Please don't try to move. General Gaius has gone for help.'

'No need,' the bear growled through clenched teeth. Dark, sticky blood trickled from his wounds into his fur. 'No healer can fix this.'

'Just stay still,' Calib said stubbornly. 'I'll find something to help.' Calib turned to run back to the castle, but the bear held the mouse in place by his tail. He twisted and pulled, but Berwin's grip was too strong.

'Why are you doing this?' Calib demanded. Hot, desperate tears began pouring down his cheeks. 'Why won't you let me save you?'

'Shed no tears for me, little mouse,' Berwin said, managing a small smile. 'Before you came into my den, I had nothing to live for. I am the last bear in Britain, Calib. I have known this for many years.'

His voice grew quieter and gentler. His eyes became soft and sad. 'I must return to my kinfolk, in a land where the living cannot tread.'

'No,' Calib said, stifling the sobs that welled up in his throat. 'You can't die. We've won the war.' He clutched Berwin's giant muzzle and rested his own snout on top. 'Please. I promised to find you another bear.'

'You have given me something better, Calib Christopher – a chance . . . to die . . . with honour.'

Snow began to collect on the bear's fur. Berwin let out a long exhale, surrounding Calib in the warm steam of his breath. The light left the bear's eyes like a dying ember of coal. Berwin, the last bear of Britain, saw no more.

Chapter Forty-Seven

That evening, Camelot held a victory feast of such grandeur, bards would sing of it for years to come.

In the human hall, flaky, juicy meat pies and smoked legs of mutton were stacked high on the Round Table. Red mead and golden lagers flowed freely from wooden barrels. Trenchers of roasted potatoes and turnips drizzled with gravy and glazes lined the outer tables. There was even a table full of sweets, from treacle tarts to honeyed oatcakes.

The music and chatter blended together in a pleasant harmony throughout the throne room. An ambitious musician played a rapid-fire fiddle tune

as knights and ladies danced and twirled in celebration of King Arthur and his knights' return.
Sitting on his throne, King Arthur beamed at the
castle's inhabitants. He tilted his head often in the
direction of Queen Guinevere as she leaned into
him. Her braids were wrapped around her head
like a coronet, and Galahad thought she had never
looked more beautiful, or more happy.

In fact, Galahad had never seen the castle so full
of merriment. He marvelled at how much had
changed from the Camelot he thought he knew.
No longer suited up like a drab kitchen boy,
Galahad was dressed in the nicest robes that his
mother had sent with him from the nunnery – a
thick velvet tunic with Sir Lancelot's crest embroidered on the back.

At his side, the Sword in the Stone hung in a
plain leather scabbard he had taken from the
armoury. The weight of it felt good, like it was
already a part of him. But it was also heavy, and
even a little frightening. Even with the blade
concealed, the sword drew stares from everyone
around. He did not know what his future would
bring, but he knew that drawing the sword had
changed it in ways that could not be undone.

As he left the table to get seconds, knights and

servants all clapped him on the back, congratulating him.

All the attention felt strange to him. Or maybe it was just the fine clothing. Galahad found himself missing the ridiculous server's outfit he had had to wear. At least in that, he didn't feel like he was pretending to be something he was not.

Galahad was debating whether he should retreat to his quarters and change when he felt a tap on his shoulder. He turned to see a tall, blond man with a matching coat of arms on his chest. His face was handsomely bearded. A bittersweet expression, somewhere between pride and sadness, played at the corner of his lips.

'Your reputation precedes you, young Galahad,' he said in a deep voice, his grey eyes beaming. 'And you wear the colours well.'

Galahad was speechless. He had replayed this scene in his head so many times through his life. Sometimes, he imagined he'd say words of anger and accusation. But now, nothing seemed adequate for a father he had never met.

All he could say was, 'Hello.'

Sir Lancelot placed both his hands on Galahad's shoulders and wrapped him in a hug. Galahad felt his throat tighten and willed himself not to cry.

'I'm sorry, my son.' Lancelot's voice was thick with emotion. 'I will explain everything in time. Just know that I had not meant to be gone as much as I was.'

Looking past his father, Galahad spied a small mouse watching him from the ledge above. The two exchanged knowing glances. Then the mouse scurried along the edge of the dome, dropped down to a window ledge behind the throne, and squeezed through a missing pane in a stained-glass window.

'Excuse me,' Galahad said, wiggling out of his father's grip and bowing. 'I have someone, to um, thank first.'

Ducking out of the throne room, Galahad wound his way through several side passages until he emerged into Queen Guinevere's garden. His breath made clouds in the frosty night air. The mouse was there, waiting on the stone wall overlooking the cliffs. Galahad recognised the circle of white fur on his right ear, in contrast to the tawny brown of his face and paws. The mouse was dressed in dark-red robes with a tiny gold goblet stitched across the chest, and he wore a needle-like sword at his side. He looked up at Galahad with curious black eyes, and twitched his whiskers in what seemed like a friendly gesture.

Galahad kneeled before him and bowed his head. 'I owe you everything,' he said solemnly, straightening up, 'but I don't even know your name.'

In the white snow that had collected, the mouse scrawled something with his tail.

'Calib?' he asked, reading the tiny letters in wonder.

The mouse nodded appreciatively.

Galahad unsheathed his sword.

This time, Galahad knew what to expect. As the sword reflected the pale-blue moon and wide ocean, he felt himself being swept away by the current of voices. He felt the dreams of slumbering animals in hibernation.

'You must name the sword,' a new voice came to his ears. It sounded familiar, like an old man's. Galahad closed his eyes and concentrated on the voice until a blurry outline of a wolf appeared in his mind. One eye was blue; one eye was green. 'All heroes name their swords.'

'This sword's name is Ex*calib*ur,' Galahad said aloud, holding out the sword so that Calib might scurry onto it. 'For the noble mouse who helped the castle in its darkest hour.'

'Galahad!' Bors stuck his head outside a nearby

window. 'What are you doing out here? They're about to make another toast in your honour!'

'Tell them I'll be there in a moment,' Galahad replied. Boy and mouse smiled at each other. The Two-Legger boy stuck out his left finger, and Calib shook it.

'Where would you like me to take you?'

Galahad gripped the hilt of the sword and focused on Calib, clearing out all the voices until the one voice he wanted came through.

'The chapel, please.'

Chapter Forty-Eight

Calib darted up the wooden beams that led to the supporting rafters of the chapel. He had taken this path countless times before. And yet, as he entered the tapestry hall, Calib felt as if he were seeing everything with new eyes.

The large battle scenes no longer looked majestic. Having seen what war was truly like, he knew the tapestry did little to truly capture the chaos, no matter how finely stitched. Calib eyed the blank space on the wall where Commander Yvers's portrait would hang one day. There was still much work to be done to strengthen and repair the castle.

And worries still weighed on Calib's mind. The Manderlean and his army were still out there, defeated but not vanquished. And now they had a new adviser who knew all of Camelot's secrets: the traitor, Percival Vole.

The mouse once again made his way to the spot where he felt most at home in all of Camelot. On the surface nothing about his father and mother's tapestry had changed. Sir Trenton still stood strong with his sword held high. Lady Clara still clasped her needle and thread primly. However, their eyes seemed to gaze upon Calib with a newfound sense of pride.

In many ways, Calib knew it wasn't the tapestry that had changed, but him. He was a different mouse now. The tapestry only reflected what he saw inside of himself.

Calib studied the embroidered goblet that formed the Christopher crest on his new set of robes. The seamstresses had used gold thread to stitch the rays of sunlight shooting forth from the goblet.

He looked around to make sure he was alone in the hall. The mouse picked up the bottom corner of the tapestry and gave it a long sniff. The scent of lavender filled Calib's nose. It reminded him that spring would arrive before long.

'I thought I might find you up here,' said a merry voice behind him.

Calib turned to see Cecily walking towards him. She looked beautiful in a dress coloured plum and opal white. For a moment, Calib was speechless.

'Everyone's waiting for you in the Goldenwood Hall,' Cecily continued. 'Are you ready?'

'I think I am.' Calib looked one last time at the blank space on the wall. 'It's just . . . I wish my grandfather were here to see everything turn out all right. See me as I am now.'

'Commander Yvers always knew how to find the best in everybody, even if they didn't believe it themselves. I don't think he ever doubted that you would live up to his name,' Cecily replied. 'He was a great mouse, and I think you are too.'

Cecily leaned over as if to tell him a secret, but she gave him a quick kiss on the cheek instead. Calib flushed hot from ears to tail tip.

The bells began to toll for eventide.

'Come on,' Cecily said, grabbing his paw. 'You can't be late to your own party!'

The Goldenwood Hall was a magnificent scene. Large picnic tables had been wheeled in to accommodate the new guests. Valentina and the rest of the crows were stringing coloured paper streamers

333

over the ceiling beams as Sir Alric supervised their placement.

All around him, Camelot and Darkling animals were working and playing together. First-year pages were learning how to box from Lylas Whitestripe. Valentina and General Gaius were exchanging stories of their travels. Even Lucinda the cat was there, purring throatily next to Leftie. The Darkling leader seemed a little bemused by her attentions.

Madame von Mandrake and her kitchen staff had prepared a feast unparalleled in the history of the Goldenwood Hall. Piping hot ladles of smashed pea soup were dished into hollowed-out acorns. Baked fish pies made from fresh sardines and minced mushroom stalks were served with savoury bread pudding made from crusts.

The hares nibbled on a crunchy salad of carrot tops, watercress bits, and radish heads. Desserts ranged from crushed blueberry tarts glazed with honey to lemon peel cakes. Wheels of fine cheeses and flagons of elderberry wine passed freely from creature to creature. Gourds and thimbles were filled to the brim. Barnaby looked like he might topple from overeating. Even Warren was striking up a conversation with Two-Bits the black squirrel, who could only sip broth.

Calib stopped for a moment, raising his glass to Warren, who returned the gesture with a smile that seemed uncharacteristically free of mockery.

'Oy, young Christopher!' Two-Bits the black squirrel clapped Calib on the back. 'I never did thank ye properly for clearing my name.' He took a sip of broth. 'Not that I care what a bunch o' pompous Camelot ninnies think, mind ye. It's just, well' – he scratched his head uncertainly – 'maybe ye're not all a bad sort.'

The Round Table from the council room had also been moved to the stage so that the Darkling and Camelot leaders could sit side by side. Every seat in the hall was filled. Only the Goldenwood throne stood empty, Commander Kensington opting to sit in her old chair instead.

On cue, the music quieted, and Leftie and Kensington stepped forward to address the crowds.

'We raise our glasses this evening not as only victors of our battles, but as mourners for our fallen,' Commander Kensington began, the candle-light illuminating her old and new battle scars. 'We gather here to honour the many we lost on the battlefield. May they never be forgotten for their sacrifices.'

Lylas Whitestripe began to read through a list

of all who had died in battle, including General Flit, Sir Owen Onewhisker, and Berwin the Brave, friend to all.

For each name, a white banner with a golden paw print was unrolled from the ceiling. Soon, the space above the arena was filled with gently swaying swaths of white and gold. The room was hushed as each animal placed a paw over their hearts or saluted with their wings.

Leftie stepped forward to speak. The lynx had cleaned up nicely. His spotted fur was untangled and brushed. His eye-patch had been recently repaired with fresh leather, and his ear wounds were dressed.

'We also raise our glass in celebration this evening, for the peace treaty between Camelot and the Darklings has been restored and will remain in effect as long as there are creatures who will fight for what is right,' Leftie said. 'Our losses would have been much greater if not for the actions of one mouse who asked questions and uncovered the truth.'

'To new friends and allies! And to Calib Christopher!' Kensington and Leftie said together. They bowed deeply to Calib, and soon the entire arena was cheering.

'To Calib Christopher!' chorused a multitude of voices.

Overwhelmed, Calib could only whisper a whole-hearted 'thank you'.

A Darkling hedgehog-bard and Ginny came onstage. The hedgehog cleared his throat and began strumming a rousing tune on his lute. He was joined by Ginny's singing. Their voices intertwined in a soaring harmony as a troupe of hedgehogs contributed drums and bagpipes:

Whether ye make ye home in stone and mortar
Whether ye prefer to roam in woods and water
Warriors are born in all sizes and shapes
No matter the colours on their flags or their capes
Together in paw and tail, lest divided we fall and fail
As long we stand together, the good in all prevails

The applause in the Goldenwood Hall was deafening, with twice the number of paws clapping together.

Calib laid a trembling paw on his heart, which hammered to the beat of the jubilant cheering. He savoured all the happy faces that beamed back at him.

To those who knew how to listen, the heart had

many important things to tell. And at that moment, Calib's heart told him that he was a Christopher mouse: brave, strong, and wise.

Acknowledgements

Firstborn books are intimidating creatures. In taming one for myself, I relied on the fiercest warriors in the land. I owe them the largest ales and my deepest gratitude.

To my editors Kamilla Benko, Andrew Harwell, and Alexandra Cooper – my sword, my bow, and my axe. Without you, a Balrog would have eaten me.

To the beacons of light at Paper Lantern Lit: Lexa Hillyer, Lauren Oliver, Tara Sonin, Alexa Wejko, and especially, Rhoda Belleza, who shone a ray on me first. To Stephen Barbara for finding the perfect home for Calib and company.

To the mighty HarperCollins team: Rosemary Brosnan and Olivia Swomley in editorial. Kim VandeWater and Lauren Kostenberger in marketing. Olivia Russo in publicity. Andrea Pappenheimer and her team in sales. Erin Fitzsimmons and Kate Engbring in design. And a special thank-you to Lindsey Carr, whose illustrations brought the story to life more beautifully than I could have imagined.

To my agent Wendi Gu, whose emails are magical manna.

To Danielle Rollins, who set me off on this path of many wonders.

I am indebted to the works of Brian Jacques and J. R. R. Tolkien. Bless the public libraries of Jonesboro, Douglasville, and Villa Rica, Georgia, for stocking them.

To my parents, everything I am was made possible by your sacrifices and your love.

To Kyle, keeper of my heart, all this happened because you believed it could.

Look out for Calib's next adventure
Voyage to Avalon.
Coming in October 2017.

P R E S S

Thank you for choosing a Piccadilly Press book.

If you would like to know more about our authors, our books or if you'd just like to know what we're up to, you can find us online.

www.piccadillypress.co.uk

You can also find us on:

We hope to see you soon!